Children of Dusk

by

James C. Struck

Cover Art by *Teddi Black*

The Wild Rose Press, Inc.
PO Box 708
Adams Basin, NY 14410-0708
Visit us at www.thewildrosepress.com

Publishing History
First Edition, 2025
Trade Paperback Print ISBN 978-1-5092-6392-9
Digital ISBN 978-1-5092-6393-6

Published in the United States of America

Dedication

To my children: Dylan, Elliott, and Ember. One cannot write properly about teenagers unless one knows and loves them.

Chapter 1

Timothy Hansen hated visiting his father. It wasn't that he didn't want to; he loved his dad. But he also hated it, hated seeing his father's current state, and most of all hated the feeling after every visit—the feeling that his father's former self was further away. At home he could remember the good things: his strong, capable hands, his ready laugh, the soft drone of his voice as he read Tim to sleep. Seuss and Silverstein, Dahl and Lewis, Tolkien and Riordan, dozens of stories, hundreds of voices, all from his father sitting in the soft pool of lamplight by Tim's bed. But every visit to his father pushed those memories away, pinned them down under glass, relics of the past. Every visit reinforced the hard, cold truth; *my father is never coming home.*

****

"It should be raining," Tim said suddenly, without looking up from his phone.

"What?" said his mother from the driver's seat. She snapped him a quick, sharp look. Quick and sharp were common adjectives used to describe Anna Hansen. She had the tight, pinched look of a woman approaching 40 who tried too hard not to look it. More than a few people thought she might be ill.

"We're going to an asylum. Shouldn't it be a dark and stormy night?" Tim gestured with a tilt of his head toward the car window, where an August sun pounded

1

down out of a flat, hazy, cloudless sky.

"Don't be melodramatic," his mother replied. "It's a hospital, not an asylum. And sit up. You look like a human pretzel."

"I'm comfortable." Tim's feet were propped up on the dash, knees higher than his head as he slouched so low he was practically horizontal in the seat.

"It's unsafe. Sit up."

Tim immediately popped up to attention, perfect posture, phone held in front of him like a trumpet in a parade.

"Like this, oh mummy dearest?" he said in a perfectly horrid British accent. She smiled slightly and smacked him playfully on the shoulder.

"Smartass."

"Oh, ow, child abuse, child abuse!"

"Please, 'child'," she quipped, smiling openly now, "you've got five inches and forty pounds on me. I couldn't put a dent in you if I tried." Her smile softened the hard edges of her face, turned back the years far more effectively than her diets, makeup, and blonde highlights. Tim loved that smile. It was like rereading the books his dad once read to him. But it faded from Anna's face too quickly. No wonder. Theirs was not a happy errand.

Forestview. Tim always thought that was a stupid name for the hospital (*asylum*, his mind piped up) where his father stayed. There was no forest to view, only a few well-kept copses of shade trees on the grounds and nothing beyond them but corn and soybean fields to the horizon, dotted here and there with a barn or silo, like islands. Not that you could see those either, wall and all in the way. No one wants to see in, Tim thought, and those inside shouldn't see out.

The guard recognized them and waved them through the front gate. The building beyond was white, angular, modern. It could have been an office building if not for the obvious security. Tim's mom parked the car and they stepped out into the pounding heat.

"Mrrrr, ho-ot," Tim whined.

"Well," his mom replied, putting on her sunglasses, "you could try shorts and t-shirts once in a while, maybe some lighter colors?"

His glare was far more eloquent than any reply, but this time he got no smile for his efforts. She just swung her purse over her shoulder and walked toward the building. He shut the car door and she pointed her key fob over her shoulder. Clunk, boop-bwip, all secure. Tim jogged half-heartedly after her toward the doors marked VISITORS.

The AC broke over them like a blessed wave as they passed into the security checkpoint. Keys, phones, all metal objects left behind to be picked up when they leave, then a sweep with a handheld metal detector, one of those half ping-pong paddle, half dustbuster-looking things, then the dull buzz-thump of the door unlocking. Standing just beyond the door was a familiar figure: tall, dark-skinned, goateed, glasses, wearing the typical doctor whites.

"Anna, Tim, thank you for coming." He extended his hand.

"Hello, Dr. Watterman," Anna replied with her best "I'm fine" smile. She shook his hand before he turned and extended it to Tim. Slightly taken aback, he hesitated for a beat and then shook it.

"Umm, hi."

3

"Umm, hi", the doctor parroted back. "Wow, I swear his voice has dropped an octave since the winter." Tim hated when adults talked like that, like he had intermittent invisibility. "Sorry I missed you in March, Anna."

"No, it's fine. Even doctors need vacations sometimes. How was Aruba?" Tim let their chitchat wash over him, his gaze wandering aimlessly over the too-familiar surroundings, the tile floor, the intense fluorescent lights. He started slightly when he realized they had continued down the hall without him.

"Before we go to see Vic, I'd like to talk about a few things first." Watterman gestured to a door to the left. Anna seemed taken aback; she had been drifting right as they walked, toward the hallway leading to the long-term ward.

"Oh, of course." He held the door open for her, and Tim hurried to catch up.

Tim had been in this room before. As he walked in, he had a brief but intense flashback of sitting on the floor of this same room, playing with some handheld video game, his mom and Watterman murmuring in the background. He flexed his left hand unconsciously, ghosts of old pains surfacing briefly then diving out of sight. The doctor pulled a rolling office chair out from behind the desk and offered it to Anna, while he and Tim each took one of the hard, plastic seats. Watterman leaned forward, resting his elbows on his knees, took a deep breath, and began.

"As you know, your husband has always been a challenging case for us. Victor is oddly resistant to the typical neuroleptics, so we've had to keep rotating them, changing dosages and timing. Prolixin was the

4

most promising, you remember, we were considering letting him come home a couple of years ago, but he would always slip back. Over the last six months, we've tried him on some of the atypical antipsychotics, and he was responding well."

"Yes," said Anna, "when we visited at the beginning of March, he seemed much calmer, much less...obsessive." Watterman nodded, then sighed, removed his glasses, and rubbed his face. Tim noticed for the first time how tired he looked.

"He relapsed, hard, a couple of weeks ago. We changed dosage schedules, but it did little good. Last week, there was an...incident with another patient. He's been confined to his room ever since. We've switched him to Fanapt, and it's stabilized him, but," —he pressed his lips together in a thin line— "Fanapt is the most powerful antipsychotic on the market, but it is not intended for long term use due to certain side effects, problems with liver and kidney function. Six to eight weeks is the maximum time we can keep him on it. That's why I asked you to come in."

"There's not much more you can do for Vic," said Anna softly, "is there?"

Tim looked sharply at his mother. Her eyes were bright with unshed tears, but her voice was rock-steady.

"We are running out of certain therapeutic options. There are others we may need to consider..."

"No," said Anna flatly. "No ECT."

"Electroconvulsive therapy may be the best option..."

"You're not going to zap my dad's brain!"

"It's not like in the movies, Tim. There are no gurneys with straps or sadistic Nurse Ratcheds."

"No, but I know what the side effects are," Anna interjected. "Memory loss, disorientation, depression. My husband is a brilliant man, Doctor, his mind is everything to him. I can't..." She swallowed. "I can't take that away from him. Not even to get him back."

Watterman sighed. "Well, that limits our options. If he shows the same resistance to the Fanapt he's shown to other medications, and if ECT isn't an option," —he hesitated as though his words left a bad taste in his mouth— "then we would be looking at Extended Care. A switch from therapy to maintenance, with the goal being keeping him comfortable, reducing the danger to himself and others, rather than treatment. In other words, if that is the course we choose to take..." He paused and glanced into both of their eyes. "Vic Hansen will most likely spend the rest of his life at Forestview."

"You really like him, don't you?" said Tim. The doctor looked at him with an expression of mild surprise.

"Yeah," he said after a moment, "yeah, son, I do. In his lucid moments, your dad is a fascinating guy. Brilliant, like your mom said, funny, a good heart. Ridiculously well-read, as I'm sure you know. Great chess player. Have you ever played with him?"

"Yeah, he was tea..." Tim trailed off. "Yeah, a little."

"We've used it as a form of therapy, or really in conjunction with it." Tim saw his mom nodding; she knew this already. "Guy like your dad, with a mind like his, we had to get him off-balance in order for the talking therapies to work. So we'd play speed chess, or really,"—Watterman gave a small laugh— "he'd play and I'd get schooled. We'd free associate between moves, get him to look at his own mind. He always throws this quote out at me whenever we do it—I guess it's from Silence of the Lambs?"

"Do you really expect to dissect me with this blunt little tool?" Anna spoke in a nasal, resonant tone, a truly horrible Anthony Hopkins impression. All three of them hesitated for a beat, then burst out laughing.

"Yeah, that's the one." He gazed down at the floor, smiling faintly, then raised his head. "Anna, I've been Vic's doctor for almost six years. I've seen him at his best and his worst, when he's almost all here and when the disease drags him down. I care about him, and about both of you, and it hurts my heart to think of Victor Hansen in Extended Care. As his doctor and your friend, please, think about ECT."

Tim's mom closed her eyes, and a single tear, sooty with mascara, ran down each cheek. "Do I have to decide now?"

"No, of course not. If nothing else, there's still the hope that the course of Fanapt may stabilize him. We have at least until the end of September, perhaps a little longer."

Anna Hansen, her eyes still closed, nodded. "Can we see him now?"

"Of course."

Vic Hansen had always been long and lanky. Tim had a vague memory of some old friend of his dad's visiting once who always called him Crow instead of Vic like everyone else. When he asked his dad why, he explained that it was short for Scarecrow, and then he had danced clumsily about singing "If I Only Had a Brain" until Tim giggled. But he had never really thought his dad resembled his old nickname. Now as he, his mother, Dr. Watterman, and a big blond orderly by the name of Al entered his father's room, Tim reassessed that idea. His father sat motionless at the head of his bed, staring unblinking out at the hazy day, looking like nothing so much as a retired scarecrow, pulled down off his post and cast into a corner, a jumble of sticks wrapped in unwanted clothes. Only his hair seemed vital; a thick and unruly mass of copper-brown waves, shot through with a scattering of silver strands, like bright dimes in a jarful of pennies.

"Hello, Vic," said Anna.

He didn't respond. Tim noticed that his father had a beard now. He'd never seen him anything but clean-shaven, but now he had a week's growth of scruff, even more coppery than his hair, but also with more gray. It made him look like a stranger.

"Vic?" Watterman this time.

"Dad?"

At Tim's voice, Vic started like someone waking suddenly out of a doze. He pushed himself suddenly into his corner, a sharp flicker of panic in his eyes. Then he seemed to shake himself fully awake and looked at them.

"Timothy?" Tim's heart gave a pleasant squirm in his chest. It was one of his dad's things, always calling him by his full name. Hearing it gave him a tiny flicker of hope. This was still his dad. Vic unfolded himself from his corner, still staring at him with an odd intensity. As he stood, Tim realized with a shock that he was only a handbreadth shorter than his dad. Vic seemed to notice this too, because he eyed Tim up and down, his brows slightly furrowed. He placed both his hands on Tim's shoulders and looked him straight in

8

the eyes.

"Stop growing," he said, a ghost of a smile flickering across his face, and he pulled Tim into a tight hug. He sensed the heavy footsteps of Al the orderly moving toward them, but the doctor murmured something and no one broke their embrace. He felt his father shift to look up past Tim's head.

"This is my son, gentlemen. I would never..." He stopped and stiffened. Tim broke off the hug suddenly, once again unconsciously flexing his left hand, and tried to turn away. Vic caught him by the shoulders again, turning him back and gazing intently at him. His gray eyes scanned over Tim's features, especially the left side, regret and remorse etched into every line of his whiskered face.

"I will not hurt him," he finished, enunciating each word clearly, like a promise. He gave that same flicker of a smile, then seemed to notice his wife for the first time. He released Tim and folded her into the same tight embrace, his eyes squeezed shut and his face buried in her hair, breathing deeply, then gazing into her eyes before kissing her soundly. He seemed to be trying to drink her in, use every sense to ensure her reality. She broke off the kiss, reached up, and cupped his face in her hands, looking up at him.

"How are you, love?"

Vic seemed to sag slightly. "Dark have been my dreams of late," he replied.

"I'd actually like to ask you the same, Vic," said Watterman. Al the orderly stepped back and stood against the wall, as unobtrusive as his bulk would allow. Vic considered for a moment before replying.

"It's different, this...substance you have me on."

The distaste in his voice was obvious. "The others blurred things, softened them. This one..." He considered his words carefully. "There are layers in my mind, of real and unreal, of sanity and dementia, truth and falsehood. There is a new layer now, like glass, between me and my thoughts. I can observe them, but they're distant. I cannot touch them." He gazed at the doctor. "I hate it."

"More than the alternative?"'

"Hell, no," Vic said with a small snort.

"That's a good sign. You fought us pretty hard at first."

"How's the woman—what was her name, Maggie?"

"Yes, Maggie Pough. You scared her, more than anything else. No lasting harm done." When Vic said nothing else, the doctor pressed forward. "How do you feel about attacking her?"

"Feel?" Vic considered this for a moment, as though it was some fascinating bit of data. "I suppose I feel remorse."

"Suppose?"

"It's on the other side." His eyes flickered up to the window, a small crease of concern forming between his eyebrows, then smoothing out. "I'm a mime in an invisible box, except I'm also on the outside, looking in at the foolishness."

"The remorse is foolish?"

"Not a perfect metaphor, and no, the remorse is not foolish, it's just...distant." A hint of the vague, sleepwalker expression he wore when they arrived crept over Vic's face. "It's all distant. Until it isn't." His gaze drifted once more to the window, and this time a flicker of suspicion showed on his face. Tim turned to look but saw nothing but a flock of sparrows flying past. His father turned and walked to the window, intent, seeming to expect something to appear there. He put out a hand and twined it in the mesh that covered the window, his fingertips slipping into the gaps. Tension, perhaps from anticipation, perhaps from fear, now came off Vic in waves, as though some fight-or-flight instinct was welling up inside of him. Another flock of sparrows winged past.

"Thirteen seconds," he said, soft but clear.

"Vic…" said Watterman.

"You need to leave, all of you." Vic's voice was strong and harsh, ringing with command. Al the orderly moved away from his position against the wall.

"Honey, please, don't—" Anna began, but her husband cut her off without looking around.

"Watching, always watching, always making sure, never think I notice but I do, I see the patterns." A cold fist seemed to clench in Tim's stomach. He'd rarely seen his father like this. "Little spies, little eyes, little monitors, can't let them see, keep *clandestine.*" Each syllable of the word emphasized, hissing the S out between clenched teeth, low and guttural. He turned abruptly and started, as though he had expected the room to be unoccupied. His eyes were wide, shiny, and a faint gloss of sweat beaded his forehead and cheeks. His gaze flickered to each of them in turn, finally coming to rest on Tim. With what seemed to be a massive effort, he gathered himself, breathed deep and closed his eyes.

"Please *go,*" he said in a half-whisper. "The glass is cracking and when it breaks there will be blood and shrapnel and…" he opened his eyes and looked at his son. "I will not hurt you again. Ever." His mouth twisted with disgust and his eyes closed again. "No matter what I see."

The words hit Tim like a sucker punch to the stomach. He felt his face crumple and his throat constrict, and he bolted from his father's room. Behind him he heard raised voices, a vague sound of a scuffle, and then he was out of earshot, running down the hall, past the nurse's station, to the elevator, pounding the down button over and over again. The elevator doors were stainless steel, and reflected his distorted but recognizable reflection. All arms and legs, hair as unruly as his father's but dyed raven-black, swept over to obscure the left side of his face, the side mottled with burn scars. Memories of light and pain, of his father's shouts and his own screams washed over him, and he lashed out, punching his reflection, pounding it, leading with his left because he wanted to hurt it, feel something in the hand that saved his face at its own expense, blocked the worst of the fire but charred it down to tendon and bone. Someone called his name but it barely registered, and now there were bloody marks on the doors, the delicate scar tissue over his knuckles splitting. Arms reached out to grab him but Tim pulled away and lashed out one last time and at last he felt it, pain deep in his hand, and then his mother was there, calling his name, and he crumpled into her arms, sobbing like the child he still was, each gasp torn from him. The Hansens knelt there on the floor of the elevator lobby, tears mingling, mourning the loss of the family they shared. Neither of them noticed Dr. Watterman, shocked and disbelieving, examining the bloody dent Tim's final blow left on the elevator door. It was a long and quiet drive home.

Chapter 2

Three weeks later found Tim and Anna sitting in front of Wilson Township High School for Tim's first day. It had been a tense few weeks. Tim's left hand and wrist were still wrapped in an elastic bandage; a severe sprain, not the broken bones his mother had feared. He had spent the end of his summer vacation cooped up, going back and forth from phone to books to video games, not sticking to any one escape for long. Hampered by both scar and sprain, he'd gravitated to cotton candy entertainment, long on story and short on difficulty. Neither he nor his mother had talked at all about Forestview, or about anything of substance. One brief call to Watterman had told them nothing new. They were in a holding pattern, waiting for permission to proceed with their lives.

"Nervous? First day and all?" Anna took the day off from work to drop him off, and so had forgone the usual primping and preening. Dressed in a simple blouse and denim shorts, she looked both younger and older than usual.

"Yeah. A lot, actually." Despite the continuing heat, Tim still wore his long sleeves.

"Can I tell you the truth, kiddo?" She turned toward him. "High school is hell. Well," —she smiled a little— "not all of it. You are going to meet some of the most unpleasant people you will ever come across over the next four years, but you are also going to make some of the best friends you will ever have."

"Doubt it." Friends had never been Tim's strong suit, even before the scars.

"Count on it. Maybe not today, maybe not for a while, but you will." She reached out and cupped the left side of his face, her hand faintly cool against the scars. "Remember, *these are not you.* You are not your scars, or your fears, or your memories. You are *you.* And there are people in that building that will respond to that."

"Hope so."

"So, honey, listen." She pulled her hand away and gazed down into her lap, fingers knotting together. "I've set you up with weekly meetings with the school counselor."

"Mom!" He shot her a wounded look.

"Just to try." Her eyes crinkled slightly with guilt. "Just for the first month, after that, we will see what you think. I just thought…" She paused. "I just thought you'd want someone to talk to, someone outside our situation."

"You go on about how I'm gonna make friends and then set it up so that in the first week I'll be known as the freaky kid with the scars who goes and sees the school shrink?"

"It's not like that!"

"Yeah, but that's how everyone's gonna see it." Tim yanked violently on the door handle and stormed out of the car, ignoring his mom's pleas behind him. How could she do that? How? All he ever wanted was to be left alone. Classes were easy. He tolerated the subjects he didn't like, put in just enough effort in the ones he did, and coasted. Lunch was for eating, study hall for finishing as much homework as possible. School was something to be tolerated, like an unpleasant-tasting medicine: close your eyes, swallow quick, get it over with. He'd had a few acquaintances, sure, guys he didn't mind partnering with for school projects, but nothing more than that. In fact, he thought bitterly, his mom's presumption would probably help keep people away. That is, after all, what he wanted, right? So why was he so angry?

Wilson HS was set up like a wagon wheel, a two-story central hub with four low wings coming off like spokes. The hub was offices and auditorium above, cafeteria below. The wings were also two floors, but offset from the hub so that the upper level was higher than the lunchroom and the lower partly underground, with windows set into wells. Students milled about the front entrance, clustered in groups, calling out to friends not seen since June, hauling backpacks full to bursting with supplies, or texting away to whomever.

Everyone seemed to be gravitating toward a large notice kiosk set between the sets of double doors. Tim made his way through the crowd, doing his best to ignore the double-takes he got from passers-by, pretending he didn't notice the lulls in conversations he seemed to create as he passed, as though he projected an aura of silence. As he got closer, he saw that the kiosk had a large banner across the top reading HOMEROOM ASSIGNMENTS and was plastered with long lists of names, each page topped with FROSH, SOPH, JUNIOR, or SENIOR. Tim squeezed his way between people until he could read one of the FROSH lists and scanned down to the H's.

HANSEN, TIMOTHY VICTOR—B112

The bottom of each page read:

ALL STUDENTS PLEASE PROCEED TO AUDITORIUM FOR ORIENTATION

PLEASE SIT ACCORDING TO CLASS

Oh, this should be oodles of fun. An hour in a dark room first thing in the morning, listening to administrators drone about expectations. *Joy.*

He made his way through the double doors, up the stairs and into the auditorium. It was much larger on the inside than he expected, a massive pie-slice room with vaulted ceilings, muted colors, and probably close to a thousand seats that would have looked at home in a nicer-than-average movie theater. Large signs hung off the front of the raised stage marking where each class should sit, freshmen to the left, seniors to the right. He wound his way through groups and gaggles of chit chatting students loitering in the aisles, the ocean-like rumble of all the voices blurring out all but the nearest conversations.

"Oh my god, I love that…."

"Dude, you have no idea what a…."

"….can't believe that! What a…."

"…doubt we will actually find anyone."

Something about the last voice cut through the background grumble as though it had been spoken directly into Tim's ear. He turned his head toward the speaker and saw a dark-clothed couple sitting in the sophomore section, a good ten rows away from him, their heads together. It was clear at a glance they were siblings: the same long faces, hawkish noses, dark hair and eyes, so similar they could have been identical twins if not for their genders. His sudden movement caught their attention and they looked up at him with the half-startled, half-affronted expressions of people unexpectedly overheard. Embarrassed, Tim ducked his head and hustled past, feeling like a spotlight was shining down on him. As he found a seat, he glanced back and found that the girl was still watching him, a frown creasing her brow, making her seem that much more hawk-like. The lights dimmed and Tim sat, doing everything in his power not to look back at her again.

The orientation was exactly what he expected. Various administrators droned on about academic crap, and some sport coaches got up to thunderous applause from the meatheads to talk about athletics. Tim vaguely considered cross-country. He ran with his mom in the mornings and enjoyed it—it took his mind off of things, and it didn't require two good hands. After that, the principal got up for a talk (by this time Tim could see the flicker and glow of smartphone screens popping up all across the audience), and then the perfunctory applause before dismissal. As everyone rose and the sea-roar of chatter ramped up, Tim risked a quick glance at the siblings. Their backs were to him now, and he noticed that they were far less alike while standing. The boy was well over six feet, broad in the shoulders and thick in the middle, with long, swinging arms. The girl, however, was a pixie, all elbows and collarbones and a foot or more shorter than her brother. Yet somehow she seemed to be the leader of the two, cutting and bouncing through the crowd with him trailing behind like a trained bull. Then the milling of people cut them from view.

Tim was shunted and jostled along with the rest of the throng, out the doors and into the long, curving hallway that encircled the auditorium. From there he pushed left, making his way toward the paired set of double doors marked B-WING. He went through and down two flights of stairs to the lower level. This part of the school appeared to be the science department. The lower half of the stairwell, along with many of the hallway doors, was decorated with models of molecules, Einstein posters, and images of inventions. Tim's homeroom was the last door on the left.

By the look of things, B-112 was usually a physics classroom. This pleased Tim; after English he liked science best, and physics intrigued him, with its Greek symbols describing the universe, like a code waiting to be cracked. The teacher, Mr. Guadaliri, was small and energetic with wiry hair and restless hands. After taking attendance and explaining tardiness rules, he passed out course schedules to everyone. When he got to Tim, he paused.

"Oh, yes, Hansen, I have something else for you as well."

He went back to his desk, returned, and handed Tim a white envelope with his name written on it in a neat, slanted hand. He opened it and read:

Dear Tim,

My name is Dan Lum, and I am the guidance counselor here at WTHS. As I'm sure your mother informed you, she wants us to have a few preliminary conversations, so I'm dropping you this note in order to set up a time for our first get-together. I noticed on your schedule that you are free 4th period. If it is convenient for you, I would like you to come in tomorrow (Tuesday) during that time. If you would rather reschedule, stop by my office, R-26, and let me know when would be good for you.

I remain your humble servant,

Dr. Daniel Lum

Guidance Counselor, WTHS

A hot throb of anger swelled in Tim's stomach. He had almost forgotten about the school shrink. But under the frustration, the letter did pique his interest.

"'I remain your humble servant?'" he mouthed to himself. *Who writes like that? Who talks like that?* Yet something about the archaic wording caught his imagination. If nothing else, this Dan Lum seemed like a unique guy. Might not be so bad. Then Tim looked up from the letter and caught Mr. Guadaliri staring at him as he talked, a sharp and observant look in his eye. Troublemaker? the look said.

No, Tim reassessed, seeing the school shrink is going to suck.

Chapter 3

Fourth period the next day found Tim outside R-26, his hand raised to knock, when the oddest sound came from the other side of the door.

THOCK-rattle-boodeep.

"What the hell?" Tim murmured, his hand still raised. Then it came again, *THOCK-rattle-boodeep*, as though someone was throwing something electronic against the other side of the door. Then it happened a third time, *THOCK-rattle-boodeep*, then a longer pause. Tim took advantage of the lull and knocked.

"Enter," said a resonant male voice.

The office on the other side of the door was tiny, not much more than a cubicle, and made even more claustrophobic by the overwhelming variety of notices, flyers, posters, pictures, banners, and other paraphernalia hanging from every available surface. Standing in the middle of the room was one of the most unique-looking individuals Tim had ever seen. He was of a height with Tim, but easily three times as wide, linebacker shoulders above a broad gut straining at the buttons of an impeccable white button-down shirt and tie. But it was his coloration that made him so striking. His hair was smooth and glossy-black, pulled back into a sleek ponytail with a matching neat beard, but his complexion was café au lait, his lips and nose broad. Oddest of all was his eyes, seawater green but slanted, almost Asian.

"I'll tell you, since everyone always asks," he said without preamble. "This," —gesturing up and down at himself— "is what you get when a half-Black, half-Argentinian model mother marries a half-Chinese, half-Polynesian football player father. I am the world's biggest mutt." He grinned, showing very white teeth. "Daniel Lum. Outside this room it's Dr. Lum, but in here it's Dan." He fumbled for a second and then held out a hand. "You must be Tim."

"Hi, umm, Dan," said Tim, a little off-balance but intrigued again. "What were you just doing in here? There was a weird sound."

"Oh, close the door behind you and you'll find out." Tim turned and closed it, and his question was indeed answered. Hanging off the back of the door was a rather expensive-looking electronic dart board with three colorful darts sticking out of it.

"My addiction," said Lum, and held up three more darts, spread out like a hand of cards. "Tuesday night my local watering hole has a little dart competition, so I was just practicing. Also," —he gave Tim another megawatt grin,— "the noise drives the rest of the staff a little bit nuts." He held the darts out to Tim. "Fancy a game?"

"Oh, I've never played." Tim smiled when he said it. Dr. Lum was turning out to be just as interesting as his letter implied.

"Aah." Dan dismissively waved as he pulled the other three darts out of the board and reset it. "We'll play Cricket. Easy enough to pick up, and luck plays into it enough where a beginner can hold their own." He took Tim by the shoulders and guided him over to a well-worn piece of duct tape on the carpet. "Okay, technique is simple." He raised a dart to eye level and flicked it forward a few times. "Mostly wrist, elbow for power. Aim a little high at first and put more behind it than you think you need to. Beginners usually throw too softly. For now, aim at the highest numbers, fifteen to twenty, and I'll explain the rules as we go."

"Oookay," Tim said with a smirk. *What's he playing at?* He was reminded of Watterman playing chess with his father, which skirted much too close to too many unpleasant thoughts. He took aim and threw. His first hit the bottom edge of the board and caromed off. The second went high and right. And the third hit the 17 wedge, and he was rewarded with the *beedoop* he'd heard through the door, and a red light came on next to the 17 on the left side of the scoreboard.

"Told you beginners throw too soft. Now, the rules are simple: the first to hit fifteen through twenty plus the bullseye three times wins." *THOCK-rattle-beedoop,* and a light by 15 on the right side. "The kicker is those two narrow rings that go around the dart board. Hit the outer one," —*THOCK-rattle-beedoopdoop,* two lights by 16— "you score twice. Hit the inner ring," — *THOCK-rattle-beedoopdoopdoop*, and three green lights came on by 17— "and it counts triple. Got it?"

"I'm gonna get schooled, aren't I?"'

"Yeah, probably. But I'll avoid the rings from now on, give you a chance."

But even with that concession, Tim lost handily. He got some lucky hits, the biggest being a triple-20 that had Dan accusing him of pulling a sting operation, but it was no contest.

"You always play darts with your patients?" Tim

asked, as Dan was resetting the board.

"I have no patients, Tim, just kids who need to talk. And yes, I'll be honest, I do use this as an icebreaker a lot." *THOCK-rattle-beedoop.* "Mostly with the guys, though there's a couple girls who enjoy it." *THOCK-rattle-beedoop.* "I decided to use it with you because…" Dan trailed off before his third throw, then lowered his hand and turned to face Tim. "You must have been pissed when your mom told you we'd talked."

The bluntness and abrupt switch took Tim by surprise. "Yeah, I guess."

"Don't 'yeah I guess' me. I would've blown a fuse in your place." He gave Tim a sharp, assessing gaze with those odd eyes of his.

"Well, yeah, I was mad. Don't you think I had a right to be?"

"I dunno, you tell me."

"What?" Again, Tim was caught off guard.

"You tell me. This anger—do you feel it's justified?"

"Yeah. No. I dunno. It's just…" Tim couldn't articulate it, but he felt a shadow of that blind, raging frustration he'd felt at Forestview welling up again. "She should've told me."

"Wait, what? Your mom didn't tell you? She let you find out when you got the letter?"

"No no no, she told me in the car as she was dropping me off yesterday."

Dan stared at Tim incredulously, then shook his head. "Want to know what's the hardest part of this job, Tim? Parents." He pulled the darts from the board with a bit more force than was strictly necessary. "Kids I can

24

deal with. Kids are easy, but parents? They almost always make it harder than it needs to be." He sighed and seemed to consider something for a moment. "Grab a chair."

Tim sat in the chair facing the desk. Instead of parking his bulk behind it, Dan wheeled his chair around the desk and set it next to Tim. Then, with another sigh, he sat, leaned forward, and rested his elbows on his knees, staring at the wall.

"I'm going to be as straightforward as I can with you, Tim. I usually am, as a rule. Teenagers may not know half as much about the world as they think they do, but they do have exquisite noses for bullshit, pardon the profanity. So I avoid the masculine bovine excrement as much as I can, and with you, I shall do so even more than usual. Mostly because I get the sense you've gotten more than your fair share of it over your lifetime." He turned to look at Tim, eyebrows raised, waiting for confirmation. Almost involuntarily, Tim nodded. Hadn't he always felt his mom hid things, brushed things aside, avoided things?

"Now, I'm not trying to turn you against your mom—far from it. The fact that she got in touch with me first shows she's actually pretty far ahead of the curve. I'm sure that's why you have a nice anger/guilt war going on inside over this whole situation, am I right?"

After a moment, Tim nodded. "Yeah."

"Can't imagine what you two have been through. Certainly can't imagine what *that* must have been like." He gestured toward Tim's arm, then unbuttoned the cuff on his left sleeve. He rolled it up to show a series of faint, circular scars scattered across his forearm.

"Worked fast food when I was in college, got hot oil splashed on me. I bawled like a baby for two days straight." He rolled down and refastened the sleeve. "And add to that the fact that your dad was involved? I would have packed it up, personally." He regarded Tim with a look of honest admiration. "Yet here you are, no worse for wear except for some social anxiety and a serious and understandable dislike of Bunsen burners. You're strong, Tim. Stronger than you or anyone gives you credit for."

Tim stared at the floor, his cheeks flaming. Dan seemed about to say something else when sounded at the door.

"Enter," Dan said in the same resonant voice he'd used when Tim arrived, and to Tim's surprise the dark-haired girl from the first day poked her head in, an apologetic half-smile on her face. She was wearing artfully ripped black skinny jeans, leather boots, and a gray denim jacket over a vintage Star Wars tee.

"Hey, Dan," she said. Her voice was high but strong. Dan stood and Tim followed suit a heartbeat later.

"Vee, to what do I owe the pleasure?"

The girl (*Vee?* thought Tim) came into the room, shut the door, and leaned against it, the chagrin clear on her face.

"I gotta reschedule," she said sheepishly.

Dan raised his eyebrows. "Already? Didn't we do this same dance last year? Who's it from?"

"No, it's not like that. I…" She brushed a stray lock behind her ear, and Tim noticed that her dark hair was streaked with lurid pink. "I actually have to take off at lunch. Stuff for my dad."

"Humph," Dan huffed. "I was going to say, detention on the second day would be a new record for you. Fine, let me just track down my phone." Dan moved around the desk and started rummaging through the drawers. "Ah, yes," he said without looking up, "introductions. Mr. Timothy Hansen, meet Miss Genevieve Melan, another weekly visitor of mine."

"Hey," she said with a little wave, "and it's just Vee. I *hate* my full name. It makes me sound like a frilly pink princess. Dan knows that." She stuck her tongue out at him.

"No, it's cool," said Tim, "it's, you know, unique. Different."

"Yeah, whatever," she said with a half-smile. She wasn't typically pretty, but the clear, direct way she looked at him made Tim feel like his tongue was too big for his mouth. She cocked her head and regarded him, and he reflexively turned his left side away from her.

"I saw you at that dopey rally yesterday, right?"

"Yeah," said Tim, and he could feel his cheeks getting hot again. "Sorry about that."

"No, no biggie, the timing was just…" She considered for a beat. "…interesting."

"Aah, there's that stupid thing," said Dan at last. "Now, let me see…" He started tapping and scrolling away at his phone. Suddenly, Tim felt a massive wave of goosebumps run up his arms. He shuddered involuntarily, rubbing his arms with his hands, and noticed Vee watching him very closely, a hint of a smile playing at the corners of her mouth.

"Alright," said Dan, unaware of the exchange, "how is Thursday, same time sound?"

"Perfect," Vee replied.

"Am I rescheduling Gideon as well?"

"No, just me."

"Gideon?" Tim asked.

"My brother. Big guy I was talking with at the rally? Looks like me but reimagined as a Neanderthal?"

"Alright, done and done," said Dan, placing his phone back in his desk drawer and wiping his hands. "Anything else, my dear?"

"Nope, thanks, Dan." She turned to the door with the same decisive, bouncing step Tim noticed the day before. She pulled it open, then glanced back at Tim with a smile.

"See ya soon, Tim." She left.

Tim stood for a moment, feeling as though his brain had been given a quick, sharp shake; not all his thoughts had quite clicked back into place yet. He jumped slightly when Dan started talking again.

"You know, part of my little speech I planned to give you was about getting out and making friends, but I don't know if she's the right place for you to start."

"What?" said Tim stupidly.

Dan just raised his eyebrows and continued. "Vee's a sweet girl, but not someone I'd encourage you to emulate. Trouble magnets, her and Gideon both. In any case," —he clapped his hands— "we're a little short on time, so I'll wrap up. You are much better adjusted than I expected you to be, which, as I said, is a testament to your strength. My only concern is your socialization and your grades."

"My grades are fine."

"I've seen your test scores. Your grades shouldn't be fine, you should be vying for valedictorian. You coast or skip the busywork, do the projects as you see fit, ace your tests, pass with B's. Tell me with a straight face that's not deliberate." He paused, seeming to wait for Tim to reply, but when just met the councilor's gaze and said nothing, Dan continued.

"You keep your cards close to your chest, Tim. Maybe too close. So here's how the next few weeks are going to go. You're going to come here for your forty minutes, we play some darts, I shut up and you talk."

"About what?"

"Whatever. You. Want. You want to divulge your deepest dreams and nightmares? Cool. You want to talk about Monday Night Football? Also cool. My only rule is that you talk about *something*. My diagnosis for you, my young friend, is atrophy of the social muscle. So think of me as your personal trainer, here to kick your butt once a week for a month and get you into shape. After that, I leave it up to you."

"Really?" Tim was surprised. "So at the end of September, I say we're done…"

"Then *au revoir*. But if you decide that playing darts and talking with the school shrink works for you, we continue. Your call. Not your mom's, not mine, *yours*." Dan walked to the door and opened it. "Now get lost. I got a tournament to practice for, and you're not much competition. See you next week, and remember: you talk, I listen."

As Tim walked back to study hall, however, he wasn't thinking of subjects for conversation with Daniel Lum. He was thinking about strange chills and impossibly overheard conversations, dark eyes and pink streaks, and of four toss-off words that didn't sound toss-off at all: see ya soon, Tim.

They sounded like a promise.

Chapter 4

Two days later, neither school shrinks nor punk-rock waifs were on Tim's mind. He was too busy being angry.

Physical Education was, as he'd expected, a special kind of hell. His middle school didn't have gym uniforms, which meant no changing for class. Not so here at Wilson. They had nice, ugly, itchy shirts and shorts in mustard yellow and green, required for all the students. The first two days, Tim had been able to lag behind and change after nearly everyone else was finished. Today, however, they would be running the mile, so Coach White was in the locker room, moving them along so they could get started as soon as possible.

"C'mon, ladies, gotta get started so all the lollygaggers and shufflers have a chance to finish. Krause, Peterson, quit screwing around. Hansen. Earth to Hansen! Quit staring into space, get dressed. Three minutes, gentlemen, and then I get out my bullwhip. Move it!"

Tim took a deep breath, stomach knotting, and pulled his uniform out of his gym locker. The weather had continued hot, so his mom had picked him up one of those thermal arm bands that basketball players use so he could stop wearing long sleeve shirts. But that only covered him from wrist to bicep. He quickly stripped off his shirt, trying to be both swift and nonchalant, but he still heard the conversations around him die as the extent of his scarring was revealed, running down his entire left side from hairline to hipbone.

"The hell happened to you?" said a mocking voice behind him. Tim ignored it and pulled his gym shirt on. Someone else giggled nervously.

"Talking to you, Freakshow. How'd you get a face like that?"

Tim knew he was going to have to deal with this crap sooner or later, and that he'd really only have one chance to not be labeled as a bullying target. He kept his face impassive as he turned, even though his heart was thumping in his chest so hard he was sure his ears were twitching in time with it.

Standing there was the expected gaggle of jocks, flanking the obvious leader, a typical Most Likely To Succeed At Life type—blonde, blue-eyed, already muscular at 14. Tim shook his hair out of his eyes and smiled up at him.

"Oh, I caught a glimpse of your mom out of the corner of my eye." He gestured vaguely off to his left. "Luckily, I didn't look directly at her or I would have turned to stone." He then threw his arms up in front of his face and pulled out his best Gollum impression. "THE UGLY, IT BURNS US, IT DOES! IT BURNS US!"

"*Oooooooohhh*" sounded from the jocks, and there were even a few laughs. Blondie smiled, but it didn't make it to his eyes. Tim wondered if he'd just made matters better or worse.

"Alright, break it up, gentlemen. Get dressed and

outside!" Coach White turned the corner and the group immediately broke up except for Mr. Most Likely, who stayed staring at Tim.

"There a problem, Mr. Peterson?"

"No, sir, Coach White," Peterson replied.

"Well then, stop making goo-goo eyes at Hansen and get it in gear. Move!" He turned to Tim. "Waiting for an engraved invitation?"

"No, Coach White."

"Well, c'mon then!"

As he made his way out to the stadium to run, Tim saw Peterson and his buddies with their heads together, glancing back in his direction every few seconds. *Crap. This isn't going to end well.* Every one of them was bigger than Tim, several much bigger. As they entered the stadium, Coach White called them over.

"Alright, settle down now. How many of you have run the mile here before?" A few hands went up. "Okay, then I'll review the course. We start here, one full lap around the track, go around a second time until you reach the entrance, go out, full lap around the whole stadium, back inside again, opposite direction around the track, stay to the outside, and end by the visitor bleachers. Remember, one full lap around, most of a second lap, then out. There's always some dingbat who forgets." Some appreciative laughs from the jocks.

"Now, here are my rules for the mile. I don't expect miracles. I'm not gonna make cross-country runners out of most of you, but I do expect effort. I'm fifty-seven with arthritis in my knees, and I can power-walk the mile in seventeen minutes. So if any of you come in at more than twenty, that means you aren't even trying. You don't try, you get to do the mile again tomorrow." Groans came from some of the assembled boys. "On the other hand, if you can crack six minutes, you get an exemption from the mile run for the fitness tests in the spring." Some appreciative mumbles at that, and Tim's ears perked up.

"What happens if we come in under five, Coach?" Peterson smirked. Coach White let out a laugh.

"You crack a five-minute mile, Peterson, and I will kick your butt off the football team and march you right over to Coach McKenna's office to sign you up for cross-country." More laughs from the jocks. "Seriously, boys, I've been teaching freshman P.E. for twenty-eight years. Taught some of your parents. I can count the number of times a student has run 4:59 or better on their first mile of their freshman year on one hand. Last one was Terrance Bradley five years ago, and he's running the two thousand meters for UCLA and thinking about the Olympics now. So line up, ladies, the longer you wait, the hotter it's gonna get. Line up!"

Twenty-seven 14- and 15-year-old boys jostled their way over to the line, the jocks pushing their way to the front. Tim found a spot about two-thirds of the way back and toward the outside. He caught a couple of the jocks glancing back at him again. If they were going to screw with him, the most likely time would be during the outside-the-stadium leg of the run, when they would be out of Coach White's line of sight. All they had to do was stay ahead of him until then.

Tim smiled. They didn't know about his mom and the 5Ks. This was going to be fun.

Coach White's whistle tweeted and the whole group rumbled forward. Tim kept pace on the outside, waiting for the pack to thin out. He knew if he moved up too soon, the jocks would use the cover of the pack to mess with him, stick out a foot, throw out a hip. He felt the beginning of the burn settle into the long muscles of his thighs. As they came to the first curve he shifted gears, lengthening his stride, settling into a two-stride-one-breath rhythm. A stitch started up in his side and his legs started protesting in earnest. He pushed harder now. Some of the front runners started to flag, but he could see Peterson out in front with a couple of his cronies. They approached the second curve and the back of Tim's throat started to burn.

Then it happened, just as it always did when he felt like he couldn't continue. A cool, light tingle started at his fingers and toes and ran up his body to the top of his head, and he seemed to float for a moment. Endorphin rush, Runner's High, it had a lot of names, and Tim could see why. The burn in his legs and stitch in his side all faded, and his lungs seemed to open up. He skimmed easily past the first of the jocks, a lanky carrot-top with a bad complexion. He was laboring, holding his side, and he gaped at Tim as he passed. Next was another, a wide-load lineman type who came up short, puffing and gasping. He made a half-hearted attempt to throw off Tim's rhythm, but he was too winded.

So it was for the entire second lap. One by one Tim passed Peterson's friends, reveling in their surprise and their exhausted tries to mess with him. Unfortunately, it seemed that Mr. Most Likely was a runner himself. By the time Tim left the stadium, only three runners were ahead of him: another jock, Peterson, and a lanky Korean student who Tim was pretty sure was already on cross-country. Now that he had avoided most of the obstacles, his mind now went to how well he could do in the race. There was no way he could catch the leader; he had a 30 yard lead and was built like a marathoner. But could he catch the other jock? Or Peterson? Or maybe even crack 5 minutes? He pushed himself a bit harder. He'd been running in 5K races with his mom for over a year, and this was about half that distance, so Tim had a pretty good idea of how much he had left in the tank. But he also knew that if he pushed too hard he'd cramp, and if that happened now he'd be lucky to finish, let alone challenge anyone.

"Four minutes gone, ladies," came Coach White's voice over his megaphone. Okay, maybe 4:59 was unrealistic. He'd just rounded the first turn at the far end of the stadium. The leader had increased his lead even more, but he'd gained ground on the other two. No more than ten yards separated him from third, perhaps another ten to Peterson. He pushed just a little harder, and felt the first protest from his hamstrings again. No more than that, he didn't want to collapse to the gravel with a charley horse. They turned the corner and started back toward the entrance of the stadium.

The other jock was a curly-haired kid, not much bigger than Tim. He was laboring a bit, favoring his right leg, and his face looked pinched and pained. As Tim came up alongside him a series of expressions so eloquent and obvious crossed the other's face that Tim would have laughed if he had any breath to spare. *What the hell? He caught up? Crap, I'm supposed to slow him down. I can't, my leg's killing me. Peterson's gonna be pissed. Why didn't the others slow him down? I can't, I got nothing left. Screw it, not my problem.* He shook his head at Tim, gave him a fleeting smile, and then retreated to his inner world of will versus pain. Tim passed him easily and turned into the stadium, Peterson no more than ten feet ahead.

He dug deep and pushed himself as hard as he could. This wasn't about avoiding bullying or proving a point or getting out of a test anymore, this was about winning. More than anything, he wanted to beat Mr. Most Likely. Suddenly Coach White's magnified voice crackled through the air.

"And that's five minutes, boys. No winners today, but hey, looks like we have some exemption candidates. Who wants it, huh? I got three, maybe four, that could pull it off. Yeung has it in the bag, Peterson's got a good shot and right behind him…Hansen?" The obvious surprise in the old coach's voice was just fuel for Tim's fire. "Yeah, that's Hansen coming on strong. Look out!"

Peterson looked back and Tim almost lost it. The look of incredulity on his face was so perfectly comical that it took everything he had not to laugh. Instead, he grinned and winked, saving all his energy for this last leg. Peterson turned back and put his head down, willing himself to go faster, but Tim could tell he had nothing left. He must have been pushing himself to try to get the exemption and had already tapped out. Tim swung to the inside to pass him with thirty yards left in the race.

"No…way…Freakshow," Peterson gasped out, and he moved inside to block Tim. He swung back out but was blocked again. Only fifteen yards remained. Tim felt the rage building in him. He juked back left, waited for Peterson to bite, then pushed past him on the outside. Peterson's face twisted up into an angry sneer and he threw his hip out. His timing was off and, instead of knocking Tim on his face, he merely stumbled. Everything seemed suddenly to slow and focus for Tim, and he felt his rage peak like it did at Forestview. He glanced up at Peterson, laughing and pulling away, and something in his mind seemed to *flex*.

****

In two different classrooms, both of the Melan twins snapped to attention, their heads instinctively turning toward the stadium. Gideon looked concerned, but Vee slowly smiled.

They were not the only ones to notice.

****

Time seemed to snap back into place for Tim. He shook his head to clear it and realized that Peterson had lost his balance, fallen, and was clutching his ankle. Legs cramping from the break in his rhythm, Tim stumbled forward a few strides before realizing that Coach White was hurrying toward him, stopwatch dangling forgotten from his wrist.

"What the hell just happened?

"I…" Tim gasped, "Peterson, he…he kept trying to…"

"Yeah, yeah, I don't care about that. It's a race, you're both trying to win. What I mean is, what did you do, hook his ankle or something?"

"What?" Tim was flabbergasted. Was Coach White really trying to pin this on him? "No, I… I didn't touch him… he bumped into me!" White just looked at him for a second.

"Do you think I'm some kind of idiot, Freakshow? Hmm?" His voice was low, almost conversational, except for a note of bitter anger. He shook his head and smiled sardonically at Tim's shocked expression.

"One thing never changes in this job. You kids come here every year and always think you're smarter than the teachers, that we haven't seen all your petty little dramas and crap a hundred times before. You think we're all blind and deaf. I know Peterson and his buddies were messing with you in the locker room. So you decided to mess with him here when he was by himself."

Tim was vaguely aware that the curly-haired jock was helping Peterson to his feet, but he was too stunned to care. "Coach, I swear, he threw out his hip as I passed him, I stumbled, and he fell on his own. I never touched him, swear to God."

"Uh-huh," said White, not even looking at Tim anymore. Peterson was hobbling toward them, arm slung over his friend's shoulder, glaring at Tim like he hoped he would burst into flame. "Kyle, did Scarface here trip you?" It took Tim a second to realize that Kyle was Peterson's first name.

"Yeah," he said, his expression going from rage to elation in a heartbeat. "Yeah, must've stepped on my foot or something, twisted my ankle good."

"Oh, this is such complete bullsh…" The old coach rounded on Tim.

"Showers. *Now*." Coach White's words were clipped and sharp, forced through clenched teeth. "All I want to see is your back walking back inside. And detention after school."

"WHAT?!" But White continued as though Tim hadn't spoken.

"Moran, help Peterson to the trainer's office—get

that ankle looked at. And both of you get the mile exemption."

"You've got to be kidding!!" Tim exploded.

White got right up in his face, a finger an inch from his nose. "Now it's two days detention, and you get to run the mile again tomorrow with the stragglers. Open your ugly mouth again and it's a week of both! You just screwed up the ankle of the kid who has a shot at leading us to State in a couple of years, maybe even sooner. Think I'm coming down on you hard, Freakshow? Say a word and you'll find out what hard really is. Showers. NOW."

Furious but silent, Tim turned to leave. As he did, he caught Peterson's eye. He was smirking, but just like in the locker room, the expression didn't make it to his eyes. They were cold and angry, and Tim knew there would be consequences other than detentions in store for him.

Chapter 5

The phone conversation with his mom did not go well.

"Listen to me, young man," she said once Tim was done explaining his side. "You need to rein in that temper of yours. First the hospital, now this?"

"You've got to be kidding me, Mom! You're taking their side?"

"I'm not taking anyone's side, Timothy Victor." She only pulled out the middle name when she was at the end of her patience. She sighed, and Tim could imagine her standing in the kitchen or in her study, gathering herself. "Look at it from the teacher's perspective. Two boys have a conflict, they scuffle, one gets hurt…"

"And their golden boy, one-day varsity quarterback, gets the benefit of the doubt and I get the shaft? It's not fair!"

"No," she said, "but that changes nothing. You lost your temper *with a teacher*." She emphasized the last words to cut off the protest she knew was building at the other end of the phone. "I am not going to interfere with the consequences of that, kiddo. You need. To control. Your anger. There are…" She hesitated. "Your temper could cause more problems than you can possibly imagine."

"What were you going to say just then, Mom?"

"It's not important."

"What were you going to say?"

"*Enough.*" Tim stayed silent. "I'm not going to fight with you about this, Tim. Serve the detentions. Run the mile again." There was a pause. "I have dinner with a potential client, so I can't come pick you up after. Can you walk home?"

"Sure," said Tim curtly.

"Should be home around eight. See you then?"

"Sure."

"I love you, honey."

Tim hesitated. "Love you too, Mom," and he hung up. He leaned his forehead against the cool metal of his locker door, willing himself not to put his fist through it. *Keep my temper, and then what? Everything becomes rainbows and puppy dogs?* The injustice of the whole situation made him want to shriek. But what could he do?

"Serve the detentions. Rerun the mile," he muttered. He pocketed his phone, shouldered his backpack, and made his way down the empty halls to The Pit.

The Pit was the rather unimaginative nickname for the basement level of Wilson's central hub. A circular main room dominated by exercise equipment, with a single, short hallway coming off it. It's main decor was concrete pillars, HVAC vents, and water pipes. All the rooms off the hallway were storage or maintenance save one: C-04, detention hall. "Oh-Four" was an official part of the student lexicon. One was not sent to detention at Wilson, one was Oh-Foured.

C-04 was a dank, cheerless, slightly claustrophobic room with beige cinder block walls and fluorescents that buzzed quietly but incessantly, and tables instead of desks to make it more difficult to hold things out of view of the teacher. The staff had a rotating schedule for who would oversee the miscreants, misbehavers and malcontents on a given day. Today it was a gruff looking older woman Tim didn't know. But he did recognize one person in the room, someone he was singularly unsurprised to see there: Vee Melan.

She was sitting off to one side, booted feet up on the table, picking nail polish off of her thumb. Today she wore black-and-white striped leggings and a Jack Skellington shirt. She looked up as he came in, smiled as though she'd been expecting him, and reached over to haul an enormous purple bag off the chair to her right. He took the obvious invitation and joined her.

"Saved me a seat?"

"Figured you might need an old pro to show you the ropes."

"Are you telling me," Tim said incredulously, "that you're here on purpose because I am?"

"Don't flatter yourself," she huffed. "I'm here because I told Mr. Hagler what I thought of his U.S. History class."

"Which was?"

"That all he's really teaching is blind patriotism." Tim sniggered involuntarily.

"All right, ladies and gentlemen," said the teacher. She had the bullfrog voice of a lifetime chain smoker. "For those of you who don't know me, my name is Mrs. Gibson. I would say welcome to detention but I doubt that any of you are happy to be here. Neither am I, so let's make the next hour as painless as possible for all involved."

"Now here's how it works here in Oh-Four. I don't yell, I don't rant, I don't get upset, I don't even raise my voice. We have what we call the Baseball Rule; three strikes and you're in. More precisely, break the rules three times and you get to join us here for another hour tomorrow. As you can see behind me, each of your names is up on the whiteboard. Break a rule, get a tally mark by your name. Three marks...you get the idea.

"Luckily for you, there are only four rules in Oh-Four. First, no talking. I mean silence for an hour. Second, no sleeping, and I have an air horn in my desk to make sure you only make that mistake once." A few quiet laughs rang out from the students. Without smiling, Mrs. Gibson opened the top drawer of her desk and pulled the air horn out. "Third, no phones. As I'm sure you all have already discovered, since your generation is incapable of going more than five minutes without digital stimulation, you have neither Wi-Fi nor bars down here. That's because we are ten feet underground and right next to the main electrical room for the school. That should remove most of the temptation your pocket internet device provides, but to be clear, head down and thumbs going means tally mark, that's why they're tables instead of desks. Fourth and final, no messing with other students. As far as you are concerned, the only people who exist in this room are you and me. Are we clear?"

The dozen or so students in the class murmured their assent.

"Good. Now, it is three-twenty-seven. Detention officially starts at three-thirty, and the rules apply. The bathroom is across the hall. I suggest you use it now, since part of rules one and four is staying in your seats for the full hour."

Tim pulled his backpack onto the table. He had some biology homework he hadn't gotten to in Study Hall, so he figured he'd knock that out and then read. Vee, on the other hand, just sat there, now curled up in the chair like a cat, studying him intently. He finally turned and snapped at her.

"What?" It came out harsher than he intended, but she seemed utterly nonplussed by his reaction. Something about her made him feel...off. Too aware.

"Why don't you have scarring here?" She traced a line on her own face with one finger, from just below her mouth diagonally up to her cheekbone. Had she said it any other way, had she been even slightly sympathetic or condescending or mocking, Tim would have packed up without a word and moved to the other side of the room. But her tone was one of simple, frank curiosity. He stared at her for a moment, then without a word he raised his left hand to his face. His thumb matched the unscarred strip like a puzzle piece, and his index finger perfectly mirrored the line of scar tissue that ran from his mouth to his hairline, missing his eye by a millimeter.

"Oh shit," she said in an awed murmur.

"Thirty seconds, people, take your seats," said Mrs. Wilson.

"Why do you care?" Like Vee, Tim's tone was frankly curious. She stared at him, seeming to be gathering her courage or something similar. Then she leaned in closer, and said in a half-whisper:

"Taruch vo ma ne'anta ye."

At least that's what Tim's ears heard. But what his mind heard was a different story.

"Because you can understand me."

"What the…you…I just…" Tim stammered.

"Shh," said Vee, and she put a finger to his lips to shush him. *"Ka taruch vo ma oholo nes ye tan feich,"* she whispered. But again, Tim's mind heard perfect English.

"And because you can feel it when I do this." Goosebumps ran up Tim's arms, and the lights flickered.

"That was weird," said Mrs. Gibson. "In any case, it is now three-thirty—your quiet hour begins now."

Vee immediately sat up, hands folded in front of her, the very picture of studiousness if one ignored the impish grin on her face. Tim, on the other hand, remained where he was, turned sideways and leaning in toward her. The expression on his face was similar to someone who has just been hit in the head with a bat, but hasn't felt the pain yet. What the hell just happened? Was he going nuts? Was Vee messing with him? What in the name of…

"Mr. Hansen!"

Tim jumped like he'd been stuck with a pin, and Vee turned her head away. He turned to the teacher and realized, based on her annoyed expression, that she had called his name more than once before he responded.

"Is there a problem, Mr. Hansen?"

"N-no, no problem."

"Will you face forward then? Or do I need to separate you and Ms. Melan?"

"No," said Tim reflexively, and immediately had second thoughts. Did he really want to sit here? But now that the initial shock had worn off, curiosity was creeping in to take its place, as was doubt.

Tap, tap, tap.

Vee was now staring intently down at a notebook she'd pulled out while Tim was woolgathering. The tapping was her, drumming the eraser of a pencil on the tabletop. When she noticed she'd jarred him out of his reverie, she then tapped at something she'd written in the margin of the notebook. Tim leaned forward to read the words.

Sorry! Didn't mean to freak you out so much.

Tim grabbed his Bio notebook, flipped to the back page, and wrote in inch-high block letters. *WHAT THE HELL JUST HAPPENED?*

Vee pursed her lips, considered for a moment, then replied. *Short answer? Housetongue and elemental weaving.*

What and what?

Housetongue. Mother language—all others are derived from it.

Tim's logical mind wanted to burst out laughing, but he couldn't deny the strange, double-echo experience of her words.

How do you know it? How do I understand it?

Short answer? Because of what we are.

Tim's stomach clenched at the sight of that "we". Before he could ask anything else, Vee started writing again.

I lied.

About what?

I am here today because of you. I really wanted to talk to you. Tim looked at her again and, to his surprise, noticed that she was blushing. She wrote again. *I felt what you did to Kyle Peterson.*

I DIDN'T DO ANYTHING TO HIM!

Are you sure?

YES.

Her only reply was to underline all the words in her last response. Tim fumed. Why won't anyone believe me? He was about to write an angry reply, but he paused. Was he sure? He'd been so convinced of his own innocence, so caught up in his righteous anger at the injustice of it all that he'd almost forgotten that strange feeling when he'd stumbled. Instead, he wrote: *Something…flexed.* He saw her grin out of the corner of his eye.

You wove. I felt it.

Wove? What do you mean?

Wove the elemental strands. You wove Air to trip him. I felt it the moment you did it.

Felt it? You mean the chills?

Is that what you feel? It's different for everyone. For me, it's warmth. Gideon tells me it's like a sound too low or high to hear for him.

Your brother too?

Of course. The gift runs in families. Kinda.

Kinda?

Complicated.

Tim paused for a moment and then wrote again. *What am I?*

We go by lots of names. Duskers. Weavers. Nighthunters. Kinderdämmerung in German. The one most of us use is the Latin version, Opacaroi. Short for Filii Opacare.

What does it mean?

Children of Dusk

"While I'm sure your love letters are fascinating, this is detention, not social hour."

Tim and Vee, in perfect unison, slammed their notebooks shut and flipped them over. Thankfully, Mrs. Gibson hadn't left her desk. In fact, she hadn't even looked away from her laptop. She glanced up at them with a "don't take me for a fool" look in her eye.

"Mr. Hansen, stay where you are. Dear Genevieve," she said sweetly, and Tim heard Vee growl softly, "there's a lovely seat right here in front. Why don't you join me?" With a huff, Vee stood and heaved her enormous bag onto one shoulder. As she crossed in front of Tim, she made eye contact with him and mouthed "after". He nodded imperceptibly.

Meanwhile, Mrs. Gibson stood, picked up a black dry-erase marker, and made two marks next to their names. Tim rankled, and Vee made a sharp squawk of protest, but one look from the teacher silenced them both. Tim didn't know about his strange new acquaintance, but he was already due to spend a second afternoon in this cave of a classroom. He had no desire whatsoever to add a third. He flipped his notebook back open to the beginning and dug his bio textbook out of his bag, his mind rattling with dozens of questions, like marbles in a tin can.

Forty-seven minutes later, he was still staring at question #2.

Chapter 6

When, at long last, the bell rang, Vee grabbed her stuff and bolted from the room like her heels were on fire. Tim, however, stayed at his table for a moment, his stomach in knots. He flipped his still-unfinished homework notebook over again and skimmed to his half of the written conversation.

WHAT. THE HELL. JUST. HAPPENED?
What and what?
How do you know it? How do I understand it?
About what?
Wove? What do you mean?
Felt it? You mean the chills?

Questions, so many questions. But despite them all, his eyes kept being drawn back to one line.

Something...flexed.

"Weaving," he muttered. That's what she called it. His mind went back to the mile run again. The stumble, the rage, the crazy way time seemed to bend. *I wanted him to fall, and he did.*

"Mr. Hansen?"

Tim looked up and realized he was the only student left in the room.

"One would think that, since you have to be back here tomorrow, you would want to leave as soon as possible." Mrs. Gibson was standing, her laptop in a shoulder bag, obviously ready to get going herself.

"Sorry, Mrs. Gibson, off in my own world." He shoved the notebook and text into his backpack.

"That, and someone seems to be waiting for you." She smiled, a kind expression on her normally stern face, and walked out.

Tim shouldered his bag and followed. Vee was standing across the hall, leaning against the wall, one knee out, hands in pockets, looking thoroughly impatient. Mrs. Wilson turned her head toward Vee and said something inaudible. Vee looked surprised and perhaps a shade embarrassed, but rolled her eyes as the teacher walked away. As Tim approached, she raised one eyebrow at him.

"That took you long enough. Did you doze off or something?"

"Can't. Against the rules, remember?" Tim sobered suddenly. "Not asleep. Far, far from it, actually."

"Good." Vee glanced down the hall. Tim followed suit and saw that they were alone. When he looked back at her, Vee's eyes were bright with excitement. Her face split into a huge grin, a shrill squeal escaping her, and she launched herself into Tim's arms so hard he staggered back three steps. Caught utterly off guard, he half-heartedly hugged her back as she kicked her feet in midair and talked a mile a minute directly into his ear.

"Ohmygodohmygodohmygodohmygodohmy*GOD!* This is so awesome, you have no idea. I finally found someone. I finally found you. I've been looking for over a year, they're all gonna freak out and OH!" She dropped suddenly out of his arms and grabbed him by the front of his shirt. "We can finally go home!"

"Ooookay." Tim disengaged her hands from his shirtfront and took a step back. "I thought I was

51

confused before, but now you've completely lost me."

"I'm sorry." She inhaled deeply and ran her fingers through her already-wild hair. "I'm sorry, I'm sorry, I'm getting way ahead of myself. It's just..." She stopped, her hands clasped in front of her face like a little kid praying, then let out another squeal and started jumping around in a circle. Despite everything, Tim burst out laughing at her sheer enthusiasm. She stopped, a little flushed, and tucked her hair behind one ear.

"That's the first time I've heard you laugh." She cocked her head to one side. "It's a good laugh. Do it more often."

"Yes ma'am," Tim replied, and sketched a little salute.

"Okay, wise guy." She was suddenly more business-like. "Grab yer swag, let's roll." She hoisted her purple monster and started walking away, all bounce and decisiveness again.

"Go where?"

"Well," —she turned but continued walking backward— "first to the lot, Gideon's waiting. Then," —some of the sparkling excitement came back into her eyes— "you want answers, right?"

"Yeah."

"Well, some things are easier experienced than explained."

"I just need to be home by eight."

"Are you for real?" She stopped dead and stared at him as though she'd never seen anything like him before. "Don't worry, Cinderella, we'll get you home before you turn into a pumpkin. Now let's *go.*"

The student parking lot abutted C-Wing, so it was a short walk for them. Now, with the time approaching 5 p.m., the lot was all but deserted, but one vehicle would have stood out even if the lot were packed. It was an ancient VW Microbus, tall and wobbly-looking, painted a deep and lurid purple and decorated with a foot-wide, black and white checkerboard stripe down each side. Upon seeing it, Tim froze in his tracks.

"Why am I not shocked that this is yours?"

"Mine and Gideon's. I don't have a license."

"Really?" Tim was shocked. He couldn't wait to get his. "Why not?"

Vee looked off into the distance and smiled, as though remembering something pleasant. "Don't need one."

"Should I file that one away under 'things to also ask later'?"

"No, file it away under 'things I'll learn if I ever get my butt in gear'. Now c'mon!"

As they approached the van, Gideon unfolded himself from the driver's seat. He was even bigger than Tim remembered. At best, he would barely reach Gideon's chin, and his long arms were corded with muscle. He wore a classic Iron Maiden t-shirt stretched over his broad gut, boots not too different from his sister's, black jeans, and his dark hair, straighter but nearly as long as Tim's, was streaked with electric blue.

"Hey," he said, his voice higher than Tim had expected. He extended a hand. "Tim, right?"

"Yeah, and you're Gideon, right?" They shook. Tim's hand felt engulfed.

"I sensed what you did to Kyle Peterson. Good job, by the way. I know his brother Danny, and if Kyle's half as much of a tool, I would have loved to see him eat some track cinders." He smiled, a crooked thing that made him look even more like Vee. He turned to her.

"We need to go before we lose the light," he said in Housetongue. *"Are you sure about this? Shouldn't we…"*

"You are being rude to our guest, Brother."

"How am I being rude?"

"I can understand you perfectly, you know," Tim broke in, and immediately clamped his hand over his mouth. The words he had just spoken weren't English. They turned toward him, identical looks of surprise on their faces.

"Fast learner," said Gideon with a smile, but his eyes were suspicious. "Fast learner with quite a bit of juice."

"Enough, Gideon, I trust him. Drop it and let's go."

"I'm your Guardian, just doing my job."

"You're also my brother and you need to trust me!"

"OKAY," Tim yelled over them both. "Stop talking as if I'm not even here! If anyone should have any trust issues around here, it's me! The two of you show up out of nowhere, and all of a sudden all this weird crap starts happening and I start…" The bottom seemed to drop out of his stomach, the color drained from his face, and he had to resist a sudden urge to sit down right there.

"Tim?" Vee sounded like she was at the other end of a long tunnel. "Tim, you don't look so good. What's wrong?"

"And I start seeing things and hearing things that can't possibly be real," Tim said in a soft but clear voice, mostly to himself. "Oh, God."

"You look like you just saw a ghost," said Gideon.

"Tim, are you okay?"

"I have to go," said Tim. "I have to go right now." He started backing away from them.

"No, wait, please," Vee pleaded. "If you come with us, everything will make sense."

"Everything makes sense, everything makes way too much sense. I gotta, I…" He turned and bolted, pure red panic surging through him. He vaguely heard Vee and Gideon calling his name before the fear overloaded him and everything went white.

When Tim came around, he was squeezed into the gap under the lowermost bleachers in the stadium, curled up in a ball, his face wet. *No,* he thought over and over again. *No no no no no no.* Not like his dad, not crazy, not seeing things, not hearing things, not bound for a lifetime of pills and doctors and constantly fearing he'd hurt someone he cared about. But magic languages? Superpowers? He wasn't sure which idea scared him more—that he was going crazy or….

"Freeeeeeeekshow? Saw you run in there, Freakshow."

Oh, hell no. Not now. Why now of all times?

"You're a good runner, Freakshow, but there's no place to run now, is there? C'mon out!" Laughter erupted from several people. Tim looked up and saw half a dozen figures silhouetted against the afternoon sun, one of them on crutches.

"Did a number on my ankle, numbnuts," said Kyle Peterson, "so, on the count of three, we're coming in there to do a number on that ugly face. One! Two!"

Tim didn't wait for three. He scuttled up and bolted, zigzagging between the support posts of the bleachers. He heard yells and running feet behind him and thought, just maybe, he had a shot at getting in the clear. But then he saw three more silhouettes ahead of him and knew he was in trouble. A thick surge of anger pulsed through him and, instead of dodging off to the side, he lowered his shoulder, bowling into the ginger jock from his gym class and knocking him flat. He ducked under a second and swung his backpack at him. He connected, but then hands grabbed him from behind, fists hit his kidneys, his ribs, a foot caught him behind the knee and he went down. A looping punch caught his chin and he saw stars; a foot trod on his bad wrist, making him cry out and fall, and then the fists, feet, and what felt like a metal rod came from all sides. He went fetal to protect his face.

"Get him up, over here," said Kyle, and rough hands dragged him back further under the bleachers. He was forced up onto his knees and slammed back into a post.

"Tie him up. Use his shirt." Tim fought, knowing what was about to happen, but the fists came again and his shirt was pulled roughly up over his head. Four pairs of hands pulled his arms back until his elbows touched, then they tied his elbows together with his own shirt. Then they stepped back to laugh and admire their handiwork. Kyle hobbled forward to get right in his face, grinning cruelly.

"You are one ugly motherf…" That's as far as he got before Tim spat in his face.

Kyle Peterson promptly flipped out. "AAUUGGHH! Oh, you gross *bastard!* You sonofa…" Anger distorted his expression. He slammed his right crutch up between Tim's legs. The pain was immediate and so huge Tim's mind couldn't process it. Everything from mid thigh to his belly button seemed to have exploded. He collapsed forward as far as his shirt would allow and promptly vomited, just missing Kyle's feet. He made another sound of disgust and swung his crutch again, this time in a flat arc. It caught Tim in the left temple and his vision started to sparkle and blur at the edges.

"You know what, Freakshow? I was just going to rough you up a bit, leave you here to rot, but you insist on pissing me off." He wiped his face with his shirt, still looking utterly disgusted. Then he held up one of his crutches. "Let's play piñata, boys! Everyone gets a swing, and then," he looked right at Tim, "then we take his pants."

Through the pain and disorientation, Tim felt a familiar cold chill.

"Actually, I think you're done."

Tim looked up blearily, blood running into his left eye. Two silhouettes, imposing guy, sassy girl. He knew them? Everything inside his head felt loose.

"You think you can handle us, little girl?" Peterson hobbled closer to the smaller figure. Sniggers and catcalls erupted all around him.

"Oh," said Vee, looking him up and down, "you don't look like you're too much to…handle." More catcalls from the surrounding jocks. "On the other hand, I really doubt you can handle me." With one smooth movement, Vee kicked one of Kyle's crutches out from under him, spun, and roundhouse kicked him in the side of the head. Mr. Most Likely went down like a puppet with its strings cut, and all hell broke loose.

To Tim's fuzzy mind, it was like watching a scene from a martial arts movie. Gideon and Vee moved as though they were choreographed, weaving and dancing through the jocks effortlessly, while their opponents fumbled, tumbled, and bumbled all over themselves. Every blow the jocks tried to land hit only air, posts, or each other, every grab they attempted left them either empty-handed or staring up at one of the twins from the flat of their backs. Neither Vee nor Gideon seemed to be trying to hurt the jocks, just humiliate them. In fact, the only solid blow either of them landed was Vee's roundhouse. In the space of perhaps three minutes, every one of Kyle's friends had run off, leaving only the four of them: Vee, Gideon, Tim, and Peterson still senseless on the ground. Vee walked up to him and, none too gently, prodded him with her foot, but he didn't even groan. The twins looked at each other, nodded, and in unison took a deep breath and exhaled. A faint corona of silver-blue light surrounding each of them flickered and went out. Until then, Tim hadn't even realized it was there.

"Maybe we should strip him and tie him to a post, see how he likes it," said Vee with disgust.

"And how, exactly, would that make you better than him?" her brother replied.

"Point. Besides, his friends would be back five minutes after we left to untie him." She hunkered down in front of Tim. "Kinda defeats the purpose." She brushed a lock of hair off Tim's face and winced at what she saw. "Can you stand?"

"Betty and Bruce," Tim mumbled.

"What are you going on about?" The concern on her face increased.

"Your new names. Betty and Bruce Lee."

Vee let out a breath she didn't know she was holding and smiled. "Can you untie him?" Tim felt

Gideon fumble behind him, and his arms were free. He immediately fell forward into Vee's arms, head swimming and his arms all pins and needles.

"I don't feel so good," Tim mumbled, as all the sparkles and blotches at the edge of his vision merged into one great blackness and he tumbled forward into it.

****

As the twins carried Tim away, leaving Kyle to the dust and cobwebs, something detached itself from the darkness in the deepest part of the bleachers. It moved forward silently, keeping to the shadows, formless, perhaps the shape of a person, perhaps something more hunched and feral. It had found the misery of the sobbing, scarred boy delicious, and the terror and rage from the bullying exquisite—but this? Two whelps with the stink of weaving on them? Precisely what its master had sent it to investigate. There was danger, yes, but look what they had left behind! A perfect vehicle, already full of hatred, such a wonderful place to hide. And to feed.

The figure dissolved into what looked like liquid smoke, which slithered from shadow to shadow toward the unconscious Peterson. It flowed toward his face, hesitated, and then poured into his mouth and nose on his indrawn breath.

Kyle's eyes flew open in panic, and he convulsed on the ground, flopping and gasping like a landed fish. He gave one great heave, back arching completely off the ground, hands clawing at the dirt, then collapsed and lay still for a moment. He then sat up suddenly, held his hands out in front of him, flexed his fingers, and smiled.

Oh, this is nice, the thing occupying Kyle

Peterson's body thought. It riffled through his memories the way a person would thumb quickly through a book, glancing briefly at the pictures. *Ooh, you bad boy! A budding little sociopath, what fun!* It could feel Kyle's squealing terror, sharp and refreshing, perfectly aware of what was happening. It would snack on the boy bit by bit while it stayed, but it would be best not to devour him too quickly. Bodies tend to break down without a host spirit occupying them, and besides, with just the right trauma he might bloom into a nice little serial killer or, even better! A military family! Wind him up and send him off to war!

"Kyle? You okay, man?"

The Kyle-thing looked up at the figure, riffled through memories again, and found a name. "Yeah, Pete, I'm fine." It looked down at Kyle's taped-up ankle. Inconvenient, but a nice touch to the disguise. "Help me up."

"What do we do now? They're, like, martial artists and stuff. How can we…"

"All they did," the Kyle-thing interrupted, "was paint a big ol' bull's eye on their backs." It rifled again, looking for names. "Vee and Gideon Melan. No sir, we are far, far from done with those two, or with Freakshow."

Chapter 7

Tim's first thought when he awoke was that he was in some sort of circus tent. He was lying on something soft, his head propped up, and above him were folds and drapes of fabric in a multitude of colors. Interwoven through the cloth were strands of white Christmas lights, sometimes bare, sometimes shining through the fabric in soft greens, blues, roses, and golds. He blinked several times, and then Vee's face appeared above him, upside down from his point of view. He realized then that his head must be resting on her lap. She smiled.

"Hey."

"Hey," he replied thickly.

"How's the head, Sleeping Beauty?"

"Hurts. What's with you and the princess references today?"

She arched an eyebrow at him. "Considering they're all referring to you, Mr. Damsel-in-Distress?" she said.

Tim laughed, which felt like rocks rolling around inside his head. His chuckle morphed quickly into a groan.

"Okay," said Vee, all business, "let's do something about that head of yours. It will be a lot easier with you awake." Suddenly the lights and fabric swayed slightly, and Tim felt his gravity shift. His head thudded again, but he also got an inkling where he was.

"We're in your van," he said.

She nodded. "Gideon's van, but yeah."

"I like it."

Vee tilted her head back, admiring their surroundings. "A little bit of home," she said. Her expression faded from admiration to melancholy, so Tim didn't press the matter.

"Where are we going?" he asked.

"Someplace nice, now hush. I have work to do, and you need to help if you want to avoid a hospital trip and all the accompanying awkward questions."

"How bad am I hurt?" Tim was suddenly alarmed.

"Well, you had a concussion, and a couple of your ribs were cracked."

"Had? Why the past tense?"

Vee sighed. "Weaving can be used to heal injuries, but it's slow, hard work if the hurt person doesn't help. I did what I could while you were out."

"How am I supposed to help?"

"By drawing in the elements at the same time. Gives the healing a big boost because it kinda brings the healer and the healed into sync with one another. I don't know all the technicalities, but trying to heal someone passive is a bear. Look, why don't I just show you?"

"I-I don't know what to do." Tim felt embarrassed

"Well," said Vee with a smile, "consider this Dusker Magick 101." She shifted slightly under him and took a breath. "You know about the five elements, right?"

"I know four: earth, air, fire, and water. There's a fifth?"

"Yeah, spirit. Opacaroi have the ability to draw the energies of the elements into themselves, separate the energy into—well, 'filaments' is the easiest way to describe it—and then weave different elements together to create various effects or make different things happen."

"Sounds complicated."

"Actually, no. You don't concentrate on the weaving itself, but on the effect you want. What to weave and how is almost instinctive. There is," —she tilted her head to one side and looked off at nothing— "some book learning you gotta do if you really want to get good at it, but it's more a matter of practice and experience than anything else."

"Book learning? Not the kind of books you can just order online, I assume?"

"No, and don't try to get me off subject." She shifted again. "It's easiest to draw the energies if you have an obvious source: a campfire, a stream, a forest, an open field, but that's not always convenient. So the more usual way is from the four cardinal directions."

"From the what?"

"Like a compass. Look." She reached beneath her shirt, pulled out a pendant on a long silver chain, and held it up for him to see. About the size of an old silver dollar, it did look a bit like a map compass. A central square of black surrounded by four triangles pointing up, down, left and right in green, red, blue and yellow, respectively, bound in a circle of silver. "This is the symbol of the Children of Dusk. It's tradition that we each get a piece of jewelry with this on it for our thirteenth birthdays, a pendant for girls and a ring for boys." She indicated each of the triangles with her thumb as she talked. "North is Earth, East is Air, South is Fire, West is Water." She then pulled the chain up over her head and pressed the pendant into his left hand. "Hold that and close your eyes."

Tim did as he was told, and he felt the now-familiar cold chill.

"Concentrate on the sense of my drawing. Hold it in your mind. As you hold it, reach out further, away from me, and you will feel other sources, senses of light or temperature. Do you feel them?"

"I think I do," said Tim hesitantly. "There...there are colors." He squeezed the pendant in his hand, and the strange intuition became stronger. "No, they're not colors—they're more like scents or tastes."

"That's it! 'What you're feeling is a sixth sense—there are no words to describe it, so you have to relate it to other senses. Now, reach toward one and tell me what impressions come to you."

"To the left, it feels like heat, smells like sand and ash. Is that south?"

"Good!" exclaimed Vee. "What else?"

"If that's south, to my right is..." he reached. "Dark, smells like pine trees and petrichor."

"Petri-what?"

"Petrichor," Tim explained. "Smell of the earth after it rains. It's a dark green."

"I'll remember that for the next time I have a sudden urge to do crossword puzzles. And the other directions?"

"Above me feels like autumn leaves and wheat fields and wind at the top of a hill. At my feet are deep smells, like wet stones and algae and salt."

"Perfect, you're doing great. Now, take the pendant

and place it on your chest over your heart. It will help you focus. Line it up with the directions, you'll be able to feel which way to face it." Vee was right; the pendant felt like it wanted to orient a certain way, almost as though it were magnetized. "Now," Vee continued, "instead of reaching directly, reach through the pendant. Try your best to reach for all four at once. Once you feel them, you breathe them in."

"Really?" Tim got a sudden, amusing image of a rainbow going up his nose.

"That's what it will feel like, and if you time the drawing with your inhale, it's easier. Go ahead, try it."

"Okay." Tim hesitated, unsure if this was going to work. He blew out his breath and reached, this time focusing on the gentle weight of the pendant on his chest. Perhaps because of it, or maybe because of Vee's coaching, but the sense of the elements seemed to rush easily to him. He thought it was going to be difficult to draw on all four at once, but somehow it wasn't. He then noticed a fifth impression, something that seemed to exist between the others, at least that was the sensation he perceived. It was neither hot nor cold, but its color seemed to be a deep, soft black shot through with swirls and sparkles of silver, like a moonless night sky. Tim wondered if this was Spirit, and why Vee hadn't mentioned this one. He reached for all five, inhaled, and drew.

"Oh, my goddess..." He heard Vee mutter above him, and the van swayed suddenly under him, but Tim could not have cared less. The sensation was incredible, like a river of light flowing into him. Every sense seemed to have quadrupled in intensity. He could feel the precise location of every ache and pain in his body, hear the heartbeats of the van's other occupants, smell a dozen different smells: gas, sweat, perfume, incense, soap, engine oil, exhaust, and something sharp and herbal, like oregano. Most amazing of all was that he could feel or hear Vee and Gideon's presence. Not their thoughts precisely, but moods and mindsets. From Vee he felt shock, concern, concentration, and excitement. Gideon was a ball of tension, panic, annoyance, and more than a little worry.

"O-okay, now just…just hold that," Vee stammered. She placed her hands on either side of his head, palms at the temples, and drew through him. She did not tap into the full torrent of energies he was experiencing; rather, she took a small portion of each and…the best description Tim could come up with was she pulled the energies apart. As she did so, they separated into strands, which she then interwove with incredible deftness.

Tim couldn't keep up with what she did, but he could sense the warp and weft of the energies. She then fed the woven energies back into him, and as she did so, the most wonderful sensation of glowing warmth spread down his entire body. His eyes flew open and he was shocked to not find the entire interior of the van lit up with flowing strands of mystical energy. All the power was within the two of them. He closed his eyes again. As the warmth continued to spread through him, he felt the energies he held respond to Vee's weaves. The logic of it clicked; by using his own power and feeding it back into him, it created a resonance, amplifying the healing pattern. The sense of warmth peaked and seemed to settle into him, soaking into the myriad aches, pains, and throbbings throughout his body. Tim let out an involuntary sigh of pleasure as the inner glow faded away.

"Nice, huh?" Vee asked. "Alright, now take a deep breath and release the energies as you exhale." Tim did so, and immediately felt deflated, as though some of the light had gone out of the world. He made a small, disappointed sound in the back of his throat. Vee chuckled.

"Yeah, it's always a downer when you let go. Sit up, tell me how you feel."

Tim sat up tentatively, expecting his head or ribs or back to object, but other than a slight twinge from his temples he felt fine.

"Wow, that's…amazing." Tim reached and touched where Kyle hit him with the crutch. A few small flakes of scab came off on his fingertips, but the bloody gash had completely healed. He then unwound the elastic bandage from his left wrist, flexed it, and found it pain-free for the first time since his visit to Forestview. He smiled, but it faded from his face as he examined the unchanged scarring on the back of his hand.

"Guess your mojo can't do anything about scars, huh?" He turned around and found Vee watching him warily. "What's wrong?"

"Are you being straight with me?"

"What are you talking about?"

"You show up out of the clear blue sky after us looking for an Awake for over a year, you freak out and bolt, run right into the Jock Convention, who decide to play human piñata with you, and now…" She trailed off and looked away from him, lips pressed tightly together. "You shouldn't have been able to do that.

"Do what? I don't understand…"

"Draw all five elements at once. Hell, most beginners can't handle two at a time, but here's you drawing Spirit when I didn't even guide you to find it, and… could you have drawn more?"

"More?" Tim was no closer to understanding. "You mean more energy? I dunno, probably. I think so, yeah."

Vee shook her head, a slightly awestruck half-smile on her face. "You're already stronger than me, and you just started. I thought I was going to blow a fuse trying to handle what you pulled for me to use. You could be as strong as my father once you're trained up. But," she looked back at him, "don't take this the wrong way, but I can tell you're a noob."

"Is there a right way to take that?"

"No." Vee laughed. "I guess not." She sobered quickly. "Tim, if you're for real, if you're what you seem to be, it's gonna change everything."

"Okay, just stop." Tim held his hands up in front of him. "Enough. If anyone here has a right to doubt anyone, it's me. You have no idea how crazy this makes me feel." His eyes went to his left wrist. He took it in his other hand and rubbed it, examining it as though he expected the pain to return. "You have no idea how much this scares me," he said quietly.

"Why? I mean, I get that you're weirded out—that just makes sense—but why did you flip like that? Surprise, I get, disbelief, I get, but blind panic?" She scooted closer to him. "Tim, what are you so afraid of?"

It was on the top of Tim's tongue to let everything out, to finally tell someone all of it: his dad, the fire, the months in the hospital, Forestview, everything, but at that moment the van took a sharp right turn. They both lost their balance and had to steady themselves to keep from falling over. The interruption broke the moment for Tim. He turned away from Vee, suddenly very interested in the well-worn mattresses in the bed of the van. Vee seemed to sense it too, because she gave him one hurt look and then crawled away to the other side of the van. She pushed some of the fabric aside to reveal the back of the front seats and the back of Gideon's head.

"Just turned off?" she asked.

"Obviously," Gideon replied, "and for the love of all that's holy, warn me before throwing that much juice around, okay? You almost took the top of my head off."

"That wasn't me, little brother." She glanced back at Tim with a proud little smile.

"You're kidding me." Gideon caught Tim's eye in the rearview mirror. "Kieran's gonna flip when he meets him."

"Who's Kieran?" Tim asked.

"That's who we're going to see," Vee replied. "All of the Seekers in the area kinda report to him. I'll warn you, he's completely nuts. Brilliant, but nuts." She smiled. "You want answers? Kieran's the best source for them. That's basically his job."

"Seekers," said Tim thoughtfully. "Seeking people like me? That's what you two do?" He saw Gideon nod in the mirror.

"Got it. We're a dying breed. Not many of us are born to it anymore, so there's always Seekers out looking for anyone who's Awake. Not exactly titillating work. Bloody boring actually."

Tim quirked an eyebrow at him. "Glad I could help relieve your boredom. Next time, can we find you a means of entertainment that involves less blunt force trauma?" The twins both burst out laughing. A warmth surged inside him that had nothing to do with healing magic.

"Deal," said Gideon, wiping his eyes. "Hey, Vee, it's up here on the left, isn't it?"

"Yeah." She gave Tim an encouraging smile. "Ready to meet a friend of ours?"

"Do I have a choice?"

"Always."

Chapter 8

Tim was more than a little surprised when he got out of the van. They were in what looked like a little-used picnic area in a forest preserve. A few wooden picnic tables, splintered and gray with age, stood beside weed-entwined outdoor grills, their metal orange with rust. At the far end of the lot, a covered eating area festooned with carved graffiti and spiderwebs stood next to a weather-faded sign naming it the William Marquette Memorial Rest Area. But what really caught Tim off-guard was the position of the sun. When Kyle and his cronies caught him under the bleachers, it was mid-afternoon, the sun only halfway to the horizon. Now, an orange-gold glow lit only the tops of the surrounding trees and the sky was streaked with bands of clouds the color of fire. He turned to his companions.

"How long was I out?"

"Nearly three hours," Vee replied. "Like I said, healing someone passive is a slow pain in the butt." She stretched luxuriantly, twining her fingers together high above her head. Her shirt pulled up slightly, revealing a strip of flat belly. Despite his concern over the time of day, his glance went reflexively to her exposed skin, his face reddening when she noticed him looking. She smiled and shook her head at his embarrassment. Suddenly she cringed as Gideon appeared behind her, twisting his head from side to side, his neck emitting a series of pops and cracks like firecrackers.

"Gross!" she exclaimed. As a reply, her brother just grinned at her and arched his back, giving off even more pops.

"Double gross!" She smacked him on the shoulder. "You know that gives me the heebie jeebies. Jerk." Gideon just laughed.

"Hang on," Tim interrupted, "if I was out for three hours..." He dug in his pocket for his phone, pulled it out, and swore loudly. "It's almost seven!"

"So?" Gideon was utterly unconcerned.

"What happened to getting me home before I pumpkined up?"

"That's before my sister had to play doctor with you." Behind him, Vee snorted loudly. "Oh," he exclaimed, "wow, yeah, there's a joke in there somewhere, isn't there?"

"Ya think?" Vee laughed openly.

"I'm serious!" Tim stopped, suddenly realizing something. "Wait, is this where you planned to take me all along?"

"Yeah," said Vee. "So?"

"You never planned to get me home on time, did you?"

"Nope," she said without a hint of regret or hesitation.

"That's seriously not cool." Tim turned away from them and examined his phone again. "No service. Wonderful."

"Hey, man." Gideon came over and put a hand on Tim's shoulder, turning him back. "A little perspective here. We just saved you from a beating that was going to land you in the hospital, healed you, and showed you that magic is alive and well and that the world is way more amazing than you ever realized, and you honestly think your curfew should be high on your priority list?"

"You don't understand." He turned to face the twins fully. "It's just my mom and me. It's been just us for years now. If I don't show up, she'll freak. If I let her know, she'll probably be cool." He smiled slightly. "Actually, she'll probably be happy I'm out with friends. People aren't exactly my strong suit, in case you hadn't noticed."

"Naw," said Gideon with a wave, "never noticed at all. It's not like you, you know, ever had a panic attack around us or anything."

"Your dad's not around?" asked Vee. Tim hesitated before answering.

"Something like that."

"Sore subject?"

"Not sore, just…" —Tim flexed his left hand— "…complicated."

"We need to go," Gideon interrupted, looking at the sky, which had gone from gold to orange-pink. "It's almost time." He turned and headed toward an overgrown path at the far end of the picnic area. Until that moment, Tim hadn't even noticed it was there. He stared quizzically after Gideon.

"So, your buddy…Kieran? He lives in a forest preserve?"

"No," Vee replied. "This is just the easiest place to get to him from."

"Vague much?"

"Just easier to show rather than tell." She held out her hand to Tim. He looked at it like it was a pet that might bite.

"You really don't do people, do you?" She actually looked a little hurt.

Tim shook his head. "No, I don't."

"Well, then start!" She reached out, grabbed his wrist with one hand and then twined the fingers of the other tightly with his. Her hands were slender but long, almost out of proportion with the rest of her, and surprisingly strong. She grinned at him.

"See, touch good. Now, c'mon!" She dragged him toward the path.

As soon as they cleared the tree line, the path opened up, broad and smooth with branches intertwining tunnel-like above their heads. He could see Gideon's broad, black-clad back a few yards ahead of them. The abrupt change startled Tim. How could the path not be more visible from the clearing? He looked back and found only rank upon rank of mature trees behind them, the path meandering back until it was lost in the undergrowth.

"What the hell?" He tried to stop but Vee dragged him onward.

"Not in Kansas anymore, Dorothy." She grinned. "Duskers only, Sleepers Need Not Apply."

"Sleepers? Normal people, I assume?"

"I hate that word, but yeah. They're asleep, we're awake. Awake to what the world is really like. Now," she raised her voice to override his questions, "you're going to feel a little weird in a bit. Dizzy, like you're turning when you're not. That's normal."

"Thought you hated that word," said Tim with a smirk.

"Shut up, wiseguy. Anyway, the feeling will build until you think you're about to fall over, then it will stop all of a sudden. Soon as that happens, we're there. Just keep hold of my hand and keep moving no matter what."

"What happens if we stop?"

"Feeling gets worse and then we find ourselves back at the clearing. If that happens, we'd have to wait a whole day to try again, so try to keep up, okay?"

"We can only try once? I don't understand."

"Children of Dusk, remember? The only time the path appears is at sunset."

"Cute," said Tim. "Some sort of defense mechanism?"

Vee considered before answering. "More like an advantageous side effect. Anyway, just keep hold of me and keep moving. It will make a lot more sense once we're through."

A few steps later, Tim felt it. When he was little, Tim's dad put up a tire swing in their backyard. Tim's favorite pastime was twisting it around and around until the rope was so kinked he couldn't touch the ground anymore. Then he would tuck his knees up by his chin and whirl like a top. As soon as it stopped, he would get off and stumble around drunkenly, giggling, until he lost his balance and fell to the ground. He would lay there until the ground stopped tilting and rotating under him, then do it all over again. This sensation was similar, except it only seemed to happen when he pushed off against the ground. It was as if he were walking on a plate that rotated each time he shifted his weight—first left, then right. He tightened his grip on Vee's hand. She gave a return squeeze but said nothing, not that Tim found her silence surprising. Within the first five steps, his already-overtaxed stomach was sloshing with nausea.

The sensation continued to build. At first, Tim kept his eyes open, focusing on Gideon's back, but eventually it was too disorienting to even do that. He squeezed his eyes shut and just concentrated on his feet. Left, right, left, right, the twisting vertigo increasing more and more. Tim gritted his teeth and willed himself to remain upright. He felt Vee's hand jerk and he clamped down, not sure whether he was trying to help her or desperately clinging to something solid. Suddenly he felt a different sensation, a strange resistance, as though the air around him had thickened. He pushed forward one last step and the entire world seemed to snap 180 degrees around. He stumbled forward, the vertigo gone, and released his death grip on Vee's hand in order to keep his balance. He bent over, hands on his knees, eyes closed, head throbbing, willing his stomach to behave itself, breathing slow and deep. Just ahead of him, he heard the unmistakable sound of one of the twins losing their battle with the nausea.

"Every time," said Vee unsteadily from his left.

"Go to Hades, sister," muttered Gideon thickly in Housetongue.

Perhaps because of his childhood experience with tire swings, Tim was the first of the trio to recover. He straightened, rubbed his face with his hands, opened his eyes, and gasped at what he saw.

They were standing in the center of a Stonehenge-like circle at the top of a large hill. Surrounding the base of the hill was a forest unlike anything Tim had ever seen in his life. The trees were vast, gnarled things with trunks so large four people holding hands could not have reached around them. Their leaves were a deep, dark green, spearhead-shaped and longer than Tim's hand from what he could see, and their bark was silver-gray, smooth and almost luminescent. But it was the house tucked away at the bottom of the hill that truly took Tim's breath away. It looked neither constructed nor carved, but grown. Made from the same silvery wood as the surrounding trees, it was impossible to tell where living wood ended and building began. Trunks formed its uprights, branches created the floor, and leaves made up the roof. Tim had never seen a human-made structure that so perfectly belonged where it was.

A few hundred yards beyond the house, the trees ended abruptly, cut off by what looked like a fog bank. As Tim watched, the fog roiled and shifted, but never came any closer, as though some invisible force or barrier kept it at bay. Tim turned in a slow circle and found that both the trees and the fog encircled them completely, closer behind than in front. If he had to guess, the house, not the hilltop, was the center of the ring. As he turned, he noticed the twins watching him, Gideon with amusement, Vee with excitement. He started to smile at her until he noticed something behind her that caused his knees to unhinge completely. He sat down hard on the ground, mouth agape, staring at the sky.

There were three moons.

"Welcome," said Vee, "to the Duskrealms."

Chapter 9

"Well," Vee continued, "a Duskrealm. One of many. Kind of a small one, actually."

"You're babbling, sis," Gideon muttered, still bent over and looking a bit green. "Shut up and give him a second to process it."

Tim continued to stare upward, oblivious to the bickering. All three moons were larger than he was used to, and each was in a different phase, which he realized couldn't be possible. He shook his head in amusement at himself; how could any part of this be possible? The largest moon, which was nearly full, was smooth and almost unblemished, a pale bluish-white, striated faintly. The second, waning half, was coppery-red, the color of sandstone arches, pocked with a few craters and what looked to be mountain ranges. The third was the smallest, and most closely resembled the moon Tim was used to seeing. Only a sliver of it shone, soft gray, riddled with craters and other marks. Vee walked over and sat down beside him.

"Clotho," she said, pointing at the bluish moon, "Lachesis," pointing at the red, "and Atropos."

"The three Fates," Tim mumbled.

"Or the three aspects of the Goddess: Maiden, Mother, and Crone, depends on what mythology you prefer." She looked at him as he gazed up at the sky. "We call ourselves the Opacaroi for two reasons. First, weaving is easiest during the twilight hours. They're a time of transition, when the walls between possible and impossible are the thinnest. Second, we have the ability to find and use the paths that lead from the "normal" world," —she made air quotes with her fingers— "to what we call the Duskrealms. They're pocket worlds, places that exist in-between. They are interconnected, or at least it's much easier to travel from one to another than from Earth to here. Supposedly, centuries ago, they were like Earth, all one place, one world. Now they're like islands."

"Thank you, Professor Genevieve," said Gideon, plunking down on the other side of Tim. "You sound just like one of Dad's lectures."

"How do you guys know all this stuff?"

"We were born here," Gideon answered. "Well, not here exactly. In Avalon."

"Avalon." Tim tore his gaze away from the moons and fixed Gideon with a skeptical look. "Arthurian legends Avalon. You've got to be kidding."

"Dunno if it's the same place." Gideon shrugged. "It's just our name for it. But yeah, this is our home. Avalon is the biggest of the Duskrealms, the closest thing we have to a city. Most Duskers live there at least part-time, some all the time. Others," —he nodded toward the silvery house at the bottom of the hill— "prefer their solitude."

"Kieran, I assume?"

"Bingo," said Vee. She popped up to her feet and extended her hands to Tim. "Let's go meet him."

A rough, winding path led down the hill, bordered by white stones overgrown with green lichen. Vee skipped ahead like an overenthusiastic puppy on her way to the park, turning around every few seconds to make sure the boys were keeping up.

"She always like this?" asked Tim with a grin.

"This is a bit worse than usual." Gideon rolled his eyes. "I blame you."

"What do you mean?" He glanced down at Vee just as she turned back to them again. She gave Tim a come-on-let's-go smile and turned back around. "You don't mean...you don't think that..." Tim stammered to a verbal halt and Gideon burst out laughing.

"NO! God, no! You really do fluster easily, don't you? No, my sister is an incurable flirt, it's kinda her default setting. I think it's her goal in life to convince every guy she meets that she's completely twitterpated with him." He shook his head, still chuckling. "Vee's been high as a kite ever since she caught you listening at the rally. She can't wait to go home."

"She said something about that. What does finding me have to do with going back to...Avalon?" Tim tripped slightly over the name.

Gideon stopped dead. "She didn't tell you." Not a question. He kept walking and put his face in his hands. "That's my sister, all in, full throttle, screw the details." He looked at Tim seriously. "We were on Earth as a punishment."

"What, like being exiled or something? What for?"

"Well," Gideon hesitated, "she probably glossed over this part too, knowing her. Our dad, he's kind of an important guy in Avalon. Kind of *the* important guy, actually."

This time, Tim stopped. "Okay, hold up. If she really is Princess Genevieve, I..." He thought for a second. "I'm not sure whether I would want to hit her with a stick or just tease her endlessly."

"Oh, definitely the latter." Gideon nodded with mock severity. "It would hurt more." They both laughed.

"Come *on*!" Vee shouted from the bottom of the hill. They started down again.

"First Speaker," Gideon continued. "That's his title. First Speaker Meneleas ko Tobias Corvitae."

"Meneleas," said Tim thoughtfully. "Melan?"

"Exactly. Lots better than Heartblood in Latin. We must have had an overdramatic ancestor. I am Gideon ko Meneleas Corvitae, and she is Genevieve no Seriah Corvitae."

"So Seriah is your mom, and ko and no mean, what, "son or daughter of" whoever?"

Gideon nodded. "Anyway, our dad's an important guy. A good guy, but used to giving orders and having people follow them. Vee…"

"…doesn't like taking orders," Tim finished.

"Bingo. They fought over something…something stupid. He is in a position of leadership, has to be seen as strong and consistent, and she made their argument public. He had to make an example of her, so she got sent off to Sleeperville to find others who could become Duskers. She had to stay either for two years or until she found someone to bring back."

"Harsh." Tim looked down toward Vee, frowning slightly.

"She didn't give him much choice."

"But," Tim looked back at Gideon, "then why are you here?"

"I'm her Guardian." He said it as though it explained everything.

"I assume that's spelled with a capital G and doesn't refer to a backup parent?"

"Vee's older than me by twenty-three minutes. It's old-fashioned, but a lot of things in Dusker society are passed down through families, certain responsibilities and…titles."

"I knew it!" Tim jumped in front of Gideon and bowed flamboyantly. "Noble lord, how may I be of service?" Gideon smacked him playfully on the side of the head.

"Seriously, ya jerk, there's one tradition we put a lot of stock in, especially with twins. Two siblings are bound together magically, the younger to guard and protect the elder. It makes us grow up stronger, faster, tougher. Also, she and I can sense certain things about each other: mood, pain, location, things like that. When she got sent off, it was expected that I would come with her."

"That sucks for you, man."

Gideon shrugged and smiled. "It wasn't much of a decision. I really can't imagine not coming."

Tim chewed on that in silence for a while. They reached the bottom of the hill and found Vee literally tapping her foot with impatience.

"You're talking about me," she said indignantly.

"Of course we are," replied Gideon, supremely unconcerned. "We must, for you are the center of the universe, dear sister."

"*Go to Hades, dear brother.*" She turned on her heel and stormed off. Gideon jogged to catch up, laughing, leaving Tim slightly behind. Up close, the trees were even more impressive, like ancient ficus trees, but even more convoluted. The soft dusklight of the moons was almost completely obscured under them, yet he could still see clearly, as though the silver bark gave off its own directionless glow. He started after the twins.

And then the crazy guy fell on Tim's head.

Chapter 10

Without thinking, Tim wove Air into a crude shield over himself. It lessened the blow but the weight of his attacker still drove him to the ground. He had a vague impression of a wild mop of ginger hair, clothes the same green-black of the leaves above. He twisted his weave from a shield to a fist and drove it blindly upward, throwing the wild man off. Tim intended to slam him into the nearest thick branch, but his weave simply fell apart and his assailant turned a neat somersault in midair and landed on his feet, light as a cat. Tim scrambled to his feet and finally got a good look at him.

His first impression was of an Irish caveman. Barrel-chested and bowlegged, with unkempt, shoulder-length orange hair and a beard to match, he wore a tunic that was either made from the leaves of the surrounding trees or designed to look that way. His eyes were a pale, sharp blue, now crinkled at the corners by an oddly pleased smile.

"Good!" he boomed in Housetongue. *"Very quick and strong as an ox to boot. All the subtlety of a rock to the face, mind you, but that will come."*

"Kieran! What the hell?" Vee and Gideon were jogging back toward them. "Did you just fall on him?"

"How did you do that?" Part of Tim was furious, and sick to death of getting knocked down today, but he had noticed something fascinating. "My weave just fell apart. You did something to it, you...cut part of it?"

Kieran chuckled, a sound that managed to be both reassuring and creepy at the same time. "Very observant. Want to know how?"

Tim nodded.

"Figure it out!"

Suddenly, the air around Tim dropped 50 degrees. He fell to his knees, instantly shivering, his breath rising in a white cloud around his face. Vaguely, he heard Vee squawk in protest and Gideon yell something, but he didn't care. He understood this was some kind of test, and although his hands were already starting to go numb, he held onto his anger and tried to figure this out himself.

He could see the weave, or at least "see" was the best way to describe it. A layering of Air and Water with a few strands of Earth, it wrapped around him like a cage, turning slowly. He could sense that the first two elements created the structure and the power of the weave, but he could tell somehow that it was those few Earth strands that held everything together. His hands felt like chunks of wood and his ears burned, but he held his concentration.

There!

He felt it, a point where the Earth strands split off from each other. Desperate for warmth, he Wove a narrow blade from Air and a few strands of Fire and drove it mentally at that point. Instantly, Kieran's weave dissolved and blissful warmth flowed over Tim. He fell forward, catching himself with his hands, and heard his friends' footsteps as they ran to him.

"Slow." Kieran crossed his arms in front of him.

"Clumsy, inefficient. I could have turned you into a popsicle three times over had I wanted to. And," —he grinned again— "about five times faster than either of your knucklehead companions could pull off at your stage."

"Fine," snapped Vee as she knelt beside Tim, "but did you really have to just toss him into the deep end like that?" She put her hands on his shoulders and wove Air and Fire. A blast of warmth flew through him and his shudders instantly stopped.

"And miss out on the opportunity to see a natural like him figure it out?" He held a hand out to Tim, smiling. Tim shook his head and took it, not really believing how quickly this entire situation had turned. Kieran pulled him effortlessly to his feet, and Tim was surprised to find that he was a head taller than the older man.

"Invert the elements, attack the junction points." Kieran nodded approvingly. "Give me a month, lad, and I'll have you performing miracles. Timing couldn't be better, either."

"What do you mean?" Gideon looked concerned.

"We lost the Southern Grottos." The words meant nothing to Tim, but obviously his companions felt differently. Vee gasped and covered her mouth with her hands, while Gideon turned away and angrily kicked at the ground. "Seems the Midnighters have some new commander, young but powerful. He led an attack two nights ago, *vrolachi* and *utari* with them. Completely overwhelmed their defenses." The strange words rang in Tim's head like Housetongue, summoning images of rolling shadows and columns of ash and embers.

"Did everyone get out alright?" asked Vee.

"Yes," Kieran replied, "and they were able to close the pathstones behind them, so Avalon is safe but…"

Out of sheer frustration, Tim lashed out, slamming a weave of Earth into the ground. To his shock, a rough column of stone ten feet across erupted out of the earth under his companions' feet, tossing the three of them into the air. Kieran did his same neat flip and landed easily, but the twins fell in a jumble of arms, legs, and dyed hair. They all glared angrily at Tim.

"What the heck was that for?" Gideon sat up, wincing and rubbing the back of his head.

"I," said Tim through clenched teeth, "have had it up to HERE with you guys talking over my head and giving me no straight answers! You grab me, drag me off, practically kidnap me, save my butt, sure, but the only answers you give me just leave me with more questions. I want a simple, straightforward explanation of what's going on. *Now*."

Kieran watched this tirade with a frown, his arms crossed in front of him. As Tim trailed off, he slowly turned his head and fixed Vee with a glare that could have cracked stone.

"Genevieve?" His tone was perfectly conversational, even friendly, but Vee shrunk down into a ball as though he had just shrieked at her.

"Yeah?" Her voice was barely more than a squeak.

"When *precisely* did you actually recruit our friend Tim?"

"Umm, earlier?"

"How 'earlier'?" His calm was much more forced now.

"Earlier…today."

"Today." Kieran seemed to swell up, his lips

pressed together in a thin line. He took a deep breath, turned on his heel, walked over to the nearest tree and leaned his forehead against it. He began muttering to himself in Housetongue, so soft and fast Tim only caught snippets—phrases like "goddess grant me strength," "idiot children," and "backsides of buffalos." Tim found the whole thing rather amusing, but the twins looked positively green with dread.

"Tim…" Kieran sighed and turned back. "I owe you a huge apology. There are usually certain *protocols,"* —he shot the twins a dirty look— "that we follow when we find a potential willworker, and when these two contacted me I assumed that meant you knew what to expect. Had I known of your lack of experience, I wouldn't have greeted you the way I did." He bowed formally to Tim. "My apologies."

"Umm, that's fine, don't worry about it." Once again, Tim found himself caught flat-footed by Kieran's unpredictable behavior.

"Still…" Kieran grinned. "That makes everything you've shown me that much more impressive: your reflexive defenses, unraveling my weave, that thing." He nodded toward the column Tim had created. "I am genuinely excited to see what you can really do, my boy. But first, as you said, we owe you some answers. Come inside, and I will explain everything I can." He started back toward the house, then stopped. "Oh, and would you mind getting rid of that? Kind of blocks my front walk."

"Me?" asked Tim.

"Of course. Your mess, you clean it up."

Tim looked from the column to the twins. Vee sauntered past, hands clasped behind her, whistling at the sky, while Gideon shrugged theatrically and followed his sister toward the house.

"Thanks for all the help!" he called after them. He could still sense his weave just under the ground, supporting the rock like a hammock. He thought about what Kieran had said about inverting the elements. If Air is the opposite of Earth…

Tim drew Air, wove it, and drove it into the ground at the base. The Earth weave dissolved, and with a deep rumble the entire column collapsed back into the ground like it was on a piston. He smiled proudly to himself, turned, and found all three of them watching. He gave them all a smug grin, stuck out his tongue and blew a loud raspberry in their direction.

"Real mature, Hansen," said Gideon, and Vee looked comically affronted. Kieran simply rolled his eyes at the younger trio and turned back up the path, and the twins followed. Tim laughed to himself and jogged to catch up.

As they approached the house, Tim saw that his original observations were correct. The building was indeed formed from living trees, pruned or magicked into shape. It was larger than he'd first thought, a full three stories with shorter wings coming off each side. Kieran gestured vaguely and wove Earth as he walked up the steps and the front doors pulled aside, retracting organically into the frame. Tim could sense an echo of the older man's weave ripple throughout the structure, as though the entire house shivered.

"Is this house…alive?"

"In a sense, yes," Kieran replied. "Argent House is…aware. It recognizes people, senses threats, supports those who occupy it." He reached out and stroked the doorframe fondly, then smiled at Tim. "Come and feel."

Tim walked over, hesitantly resting his hand on the frame before closing his eyes. The wood was pleasantly warm, as though it had been sitting in the sun, and seemed to almost hum under his hand. His mind then filled with a series of gentle but strong impressions: slow growth and deep, cool earth, a thousand leaves spread like imploring hands to catch the light of the moons, and an ancient and quiet consciousness, vibrant but slow as the turn of seasons.

"It's so old," he said, "and it's everywhere." He opened his eyes and looked at Kieran. "It's not just the house, is it? It's the whole grove, all the trees."

"Yes, very good!" Kieran patted the frame. "No one knows how old Argent House is, or who created it, if any person did at all. It shows up in some of our oldest legends, so it most likely predates Dusker society completely. You're also right about the argos trees—they're all interconnected. They are really just one vast tree, and the house is an extension, an outgrowth, if you will."

"But how? They're just trees."

"And trees are just cells, and cells are just atoms, no different from the bits of carbon and nitrogen and oxygen and such that make up your own body. Yet you can bend the elements to your will, twist the fabric of reality with a thought. Are you really so arrogant as to think that such miracles are the sole province of humanity?"

"I never thought about it that way," said Tim.

"Of course you didn't." He smiled up at Tim through his beard. "You were never taught to think otherwise. Luckily, now is the best time to start changing that. Now is the *only* time to start, actually." He wiggled his eyebrows at Tim, gave his creepy-contagious laugh, and walked inside.

"Told ya," said Vee as she walked up from behind Tim. "Brilliant, but completely nuts." She smiled fondly at Kieran's retreating back.

"Yeah, that does sum him up, doesn't it?"

"C'mon," said Gideon as he joined them. "We'll show you around the place."

Tim expected the inside of Argent House to be like the outside, a place of silver and shadow, but he was wrong. His first impression upon walking through the double doors was *warm.* Every surface, every wall, every inch glowed with the deep, soft light of old wood lovingly maintained. Palest cream, deep gold, ruddy cherry, soft umber, every tone and shade possible, all polished, oiled, and worn by countless generations of Dusker inhabitants. There were no sharp edges anywhere, no beveling or chisel marks, only the sinuous curves, arcs, and rounded surfaces of living trees. Some objects, tables and chairs, had the look of human creation, but most of the larger fixtures seemed to have grown just like the rest of the house. But unlike the outside, where the silver armor of the argos trees dominated, in here was their golden heart.

The entryway opened onto a broad, high-ceilinged hall with a massive sandstone fireplace ahead, flanked by a pair of curving staircases that led to a balcony lost in shadow. Thick wooden pillars, or perhaps trunks, supported the ceiling. To the right was a series of long plank tables, enough to seat several dozen people, to the left was what looked like a library, floor-to-ceiling shelves crammed to overflowing with tomes of every size, color, and thickness, interspaced with cases and racks of strange instruments. Vine-motif sconces jutted from the pillar-trunks, each cupping a flame that had neither source nor fuel. Tim wandered closer and found that they were not flames, but spheres of light hanging unsupported in each sconce.

"They're called aetherlights," said Vee as she trailed behind him. "They respond to the presence of anyone who can willwork, and much safer than open flames in a wooden house."

Just then, Kieran bustled up carrying a tray laden with mugs, a kettle, and a basket covered with a cloth. A sweet, baked smell arose from the basket, and Tim's stomach lurched with hunger.

"Well, come come come." Kieran gestured with his head. "Much to talk about, and talk always goes better with food and drink." He moved toward the fireplace, which was surrounded by an assortment of mismatched but comfortable-looking furniture. Vee chose a low, round seat and curled up in it like a cat, gazing happily at the fire. Gideon lounged on a loveseat, his big feet dangling over one arm. Tim picked a large, high-backed chair, between the twins but further back.

"You don't have to sit so far away," said Kieran as he set the tray down on a nearby coffee table.

"Sorry," said Tim softly, "not real fond of fireplaces."

"Understandable." Kieran nodded, and busied himself with the mugs and kettle, saying nothing more, but Tim saw Vee's eyes flicker toward him, and Gideon suddenly found his left thumbnail fascinating. He knew what they wanted, but he wasn't ready to talk about that. Not yet.

As Kieran worked, a heady, almost floral scent filled the room. He brought the first mug over to Tim.

"No thanks, I'm not much of a tea drinker."

"You haven't tried this." Kieran held out the mug. "Trust me."

Tim gave him a doubtful look, but took the proffered mug. It was a thick, heavy thing, simple but not crude, and the deep warmth felt good in Tim's hands. He took a small sip. The tea was herbal, slightly sweet with a not-unpleasant bitterness underneath, but as he swallowed the most amazing crackling warmth spread from his stomach to every inch of his body, almost like how drawing the elements felt. He gasped involuntarily.

"Holy crap, what is this stuff?" Tim took another, larger sip.

"Easy there." Kieran laughed. "Go slow, you're not used to it. We call it kickapoo tea." He handed a second mug to Gideon, who grabbed at it like a greedy kid. "The plants are infused with energizing weaves as they grow. Think of it as Opacaroi caffeine." He handed a mug to Vee, who snapped it up as enthusiastically as her brother had, and then took one for himself.

Tim drank again, slowly, trying to pay close attention to the sensation. Sure enough, he felt filaments of all five elements flooding him as he swallowed. Once he got over the initial jolt, the feeling was less like a caffeine buzz and more like the deep energy from a good, healthy meal. He grinned at Kieran over the rim of his mug, who responded with a salute of his own before taking a long, hearty drink. As he did, Tim could feel the energy coming off of the older man like a static charge.

"Jeeze, Kieran!" Gideon laughed. "Careful, you're gonna blow a fuse!" In response, Kieran raised one eyebrow and belched resonantly. All three teenagers burst out laughing.

"In any case," Kieran continued with a smile, "our friend Tim has many questions." He turned and picked up the basket. "I will answer whatever I can. Scone?" He removed the cloth with a flourish and offered it to Tim. It was piled high with lumpy pastries, steaming slightly. Tim took three and crammed one into his mouth, hot and crumbly and flavored with cinnamon and dried fruit. The others helped themselves before Kieran pulled a fourth chair over between Vee and the fire, turning it to face Tim. "Where should we start?"

Tim swallowed and thought for a moment. "I dunno, they've told me a lot of disconnected stuff, about weaving, Avalon, Seekers, and so on, but I don't have the big picture. What are Duskers? Where did you, I mean, we come from? And," —Tim hesitated and licked his lips— "what exactly am I signing up for here?"

Kieran gave both of the twins the same death glare he'd used before. Gideon shook his head and wordlessly gestured toward his sister, who did her best to hide behind her mug. Kieran sighed and took another sip of his tea.

"Alright," he said, "let's take it from the top."

Chapter 11

"The world, all of existence, is a far more fragile thing than people realize, and there is far more to it than most people ever see." Kieran leaned in closer to Tim. "All. The stories. Are true."

"What do you mean?"

"Fables, fairy tales, horror stories, all the strange and fantastical creatures and powers you've read or heard about—they're all real. Angels, demons, dragons, giants, vampires, werewolves, faeries, ghosts, gods, they all exist, in one form or another, in one realm or another, and they all have an effect on the human world. More importantly for this discussion, some people are born with the ability to see more and even influence this hidden world than others. Call it what you will: magick, weaving, willworking, conscious manipulation of the zero-point field, doesn't matter. The important point is that magick exists, some people can do it, and having this ability draws you into this world of hidden things and makes you a part of it."

Tim considered this for a moment. "Have they, I mean, we always existed?"

"Haven't stories of witches and warlocks always existed? The ability has always been rare; it's a double recessive gene as best as we can figure. However, there seems to be some sort of subliminal attraction, something that draws the parents together, because there are more of us than you'd expect from that. Not a lot, perhaps a few thousand in the world, but every year Seekers bring a few more, and of course the children of two Duskers almost always have the ability, usually very strong."

Kieran paused and took a drink, then gazed into his mug and rolled it back and forth between his hands a few times before continuing.

"There were more of us once, far more. Go back five hundred years and there were easily twice as many willworkers in the world, with a human population one-tenth the size. It was then, during the Renaissance that we started to organize ourselves. The world was shrinking, Europe was exploring the Americas, cultures with no common ground were colliding, and something needed to be done to keep some semblance of peace in the world. So the willworkers of the time called a great meeting, the Grand Council they called it, and organized everyone into three houses based upon abilities, proclivities, and location in the world.

"First were the Children of Dawn, or the Avgaens, whose province was the divine forces and spirits of order. With so many cultures and philosophies being thrust together by the Age of Exploration, something needed to be done to mediate between both the followers and the pantheons themselves. They were the negotiators, the mediators, the priests and clergy, and those skilled in the Light element." He read the surprise on Tim's face. "Yes, there are actually seven elements, not five. Light and Darkness are elements too, but their use can only be taught, not discovered, and any talent in them is exceedingly rare in this day and age. Light is the element of life and the divine, Darkness the element of entropy and the infernal.

"The second, as you can probably guess, were the Children of Midnight, der Mitternachten. Demons and monsters are just as real as gods and angels, but they can't be dealt with in the same ways. Mediation just isn't possible with the infernal forces of the universe because they only want one thing: chaos. They are the avatars of entropy, and tend not to be too picky about the details of the destruction they crave. All the conflict between nations and cultures was creating chaos throughout the world, and a group was needed to stem that tide. Midnighters were warriors, pure and simple, whose job it was to keep the divine, infernal, supernatural, and human elements apart and at bay, by whatever means necessary. They recruited those with a military background and those with skill in Darkness, partly for its destructive capability, partly because of its usefulness in combating the infernal.

"Third, obviously, were the Children of Dusk. Ours was the province of all the other supernatural creatures. Sometimes it was to protect humans from these beings, sometimes the other way around, sometimes even to protect creatures from the forces of light or darkness. Because many supernatural creatures have an affinity for one element or another, Duskers tend to have skill in the primary five elements and have always prized broad skills and open minds.

"Dawn to negotiate, Dusk to defend, Midnight to enforce. The Grand Council had sky-high expectations. They honestly believed that, through cooperation and division of the metaphysical world, they would bring about a world of unprecedented peace." He looked up at Tim, the flickering shadows making his face look sinister.

"Needless to say, things did not go as planned."

"What happened?"

"Arrogance," said Kieran simply. "They only considered their ability to influence the supernatural world. It never occurred to them that the supernatural could affect us." He took another drink. "Surprisingly, it was the Dawn House that was the first to fall. Western religions have always had a xenophobic streak. Couple it with the dominance of Europe throughout that era and you can see how easy it would be to convert the scholars and negotiators into dogmatists and inquisitors. The Western-influenced Avgaens purged all other ideologies and morphed into an extension of the Spanish Inquisition, eventually turning against their own members in their phobia of all things supernatural. To the best of our knowledge, the last remnants of the Children of Dawn died out during the Enlightenment."

"If anything, the fate of the Mitternachten was worse."

"They were corrupted, weren't they?"

"Yes." Kieran raised his eyebrows. "Did they tell you about that?"

"Mitternachten, Midnighters, I can put two and two together." He gave Kieran a sarcastic smile. "I do have ears, you know."

"Point taken. I do tend to get a little pedantic when I talk about this stuff."

"He used to teach in Avalon," said Gideon, "right, K?"

"Long time ago." He gazed at the floor, a small, sad smile curving up the corners of his beard.

"What happened?" The words were out of Tim's

mouth before he realized he might be prying. "If you don't mind me asking." The older man stared at him for a moment.

"I don't mind, but it's a long story, and your education is a bit more important than my drama. Some other time?"

"Sure." Tim nodded.

"In any case…" Kieran leaned forward, set his mug on the coffee table and poured himself a refill. "It started in the mid-19th century. Some say it was the corrupting influence of Darkness weaving, some say it was the loss of balance in the world from the fall of the Avgaen. I think it was changes in the Sleeper world, personally, but who knows. All that matters is that between then and World War I, the Children of Midnight slowly rotted from the inside out, devoured by the very forces they were supposed to fight. The first half of the 20th century was the culmination: millions slaughtered over a nothing conflict, Europe decimated, sent into an economic tailspin, then the horrors of World War II, all orchestrated by the Mitternachten. The Opacaroi of the time did all they could to help the Allies. Roosevelt was one of ours, actually."

"You're kidding! FDR was a Dusker?"

"What, you actually thought his illness was polio?" Kieran shook his head. "Magickal curse from a Midnighter assassin when he was young. Their auguries caught onto the role he was destined to play—tried to kill him before he could fulfill it. So was Kennedy, but that assassination worked. We've never had that level of influence again. So many died in the wars, so many left because of what they experienced that our society all but collapsed. Human hubris, infernal corruption, and divine rigidity have run rampant through the world ever since, and you can see the result. We are too few and the forces arrayed against us are too many, but we have to stand our ground because without our small influence the world would have destroyed itself years ago. The Mitternachten now assault us directly, attacking the Duskrealms. Fewer and fewer Duskers have children now. We are the last guardians, manning the walls of a crumbling kingdom, yet we must do what we can. And that," Kieran gestured toward the twins, "is where your friends come in."

"Those we can spare, mostly young people, become Seekers. They go out into the Sleeper world to search for potentials, individuals with the ability to learn how to weave the elements. They scour the schools because the younger you are, the less calcified your beliefs, the better the chance that you are still open to the possibility of magick in the world. Potentials tend to be the outcasts, the creatives, the strange ones at the fringes of the acceptable, respectable world. Whether that sort of personality makes one more open to willworking or the gift tends to foster an outsider mentality, I'm not sure. Probably a little of both."

"Seekers *usually*," —he cast another glare at the twins— "introduce potentials to this world slowly, let them get used to the idea and learn their strengths. But while what these two did with you was unorthodox to say the least, I cannot fault them for their excitement."

"Why? What's so special about me?"

"Dude." Gideon sat up and leaned in toward Tim, elbows on knees. "You do things instinctually that normally take people months to learn, stuff that even Vee and I couldn't get that fast, and we were born

Duskers. That's why I was kinda hesitant about you at first."

"What—did you think I was a Midnighter in disguise or something?"

"Yeah, he did," said Vee, and her brother shot her a dirty look. "What, you did!"

"So did you, Vee," Tim cut into the middle of their budding argument. "That's why you got all weird after you healed me."

"Healed you?" Kieran looked concerned. "From what?"

"He got jumped by some jocks, beat him up pretty bad. Luckily we were there to bail him out." Vee sat up and leaned in toward Kieran. "K, he can draw all five already."

Kieran gave her an incredulous look, then got up out of his chair and crouched down in front of Tim, holding out his hands.

"Show me."

Tim shrugged and took the older man's hands. He closed his eyes, breathed out, and reached. Immediately, all the elements were there, shimmering at the edge of his consciousness, ready to be used. He drew hard on all five, feeling a puckish urge to show off a little, and started weaving, making it up as he went, layering the elements together almost by whim. He felt a little how he imagined Jackson Pollack must've felt, splattering and scribbling away on his massive canvases. Layer upon layer, finer and finer detail, he pushed his concentration to the limit, his eyes rolling back in his head.

"Tim, what are you....oh my goddess." Vee's voice dropped to a hushed whisper, tinged with awe.

"Whoa," muttered Gideon.

Tim slowly opened his eyes, still concentrating with all his might on holding the dozens of elemental threads in place. Hanging in the gloom above them was a massive spiral of light, a fractal pattern twenty feet across, shining with all the colors of the rainbow and then some. The twins gazed raptly up at it, the colors playing across their faces like Christmas lights, and even Kieran seemed impressed. He looked at Tim with a mixture of pride, amusement, and consternation.

"Very pretty, but I'd rather you not make something like that inside my house. Release the layers *slowly*, otherwise that thing is going to go off like a skyrocket."

"Sorry," Tim managed to gasp out. He didn't want to let them know how drained he already felt. Ever so slowly, he let the threads go, and the spiral shimmered apart into thousands of motes of light, drifting down onto their heads like rainbow dust. He released the last as a soft gust of Air, and the motes scattered and blinked into nothingness.

"Showoff," muttered Kieran. He released Tim's hands, picked up his mug and handed it to him. "Drink, you'll need that."

"Thanks." Tim took a large swig and almost spit it back out. The tea was still piping hot, almost as hot as when Kieran had poured it. The twins both chuckled at his discomfort, but Kieran turned and stared into the flames, seemingly lost in thought.

"Tim," he said after a moment, "do you know anything about your family tree?"

"Not really, no. My parents were both only children and my grandparents all passed before I was born. Why?"

"Well, with talent like yours, you've got to have some Denier blood on both sides."

"Some what blood?"

"Denier," said Gideon. "People who leave Dusker society forever and try to have a normal life. It usually doesn't end well."

"Why wouldn't it?"

"Think about it, Tim," said Vee. "How does weaving make you feel?"

Tim thought back to that moment in the van, the incredible, euphoric rush of the energies, the deflated sensation afterward.

"It's addictive, isn't it?"

"Yes, but it's more than that." Kieran turned away from the fireplace. "Haven't you asked yourself yet why the rest of the world doesn't know that all of this exists?"

"Well…" Tim rubbed the back of his head. All of this had happened so fast that he hadn't even considered that. "I just kinda assumed that it's really rare, the ability to weave. You said there aren't very many of us."

"You're right; that's part of it, but not all." Kieran walked back over and sat, chewing on his lip and staring at the floor. He seemed to be debating something. Finally he looked up at Tim.

"Okay, gonna get a little esoteric here, so try to keep up. Do you know anything about quantum mechanics?"

"Actually, yeah." Tim was amused at the look of surprise on Kieran's face. "I love science. I read a bunch of books on quantum mechanics. Weird stuff, but really cool: wave functions and non-locality and how the act of observing something changes it, that experiment with electrons behaving like waves until they're measured and then they become particles."

Kieran snapped his fingers and pointed at Tim. "Yes, Feynman's double-slit experiment, that's the one! He showed that matter is affected by observation. There are even experiments showing that animals can do the same. This is how we think willworking works. Some people inherit the ability to manipulate this effect consciously, to literally bend matter and energy as an act of will." He took a swig of tea before continuing. "Now, think about this. If multiple beings observe a single thing, what happens?"

Tim thought for a moment. "I'd think that it would kinda solidify things, set them in place even more."

"Ha!" Kieran gave the twins a triumphant stare. "You two need to hang out with this one more, maybe he'll rub off on you."

"Hey," said Vee, "I weave stuff, things happen. I don't really care why." Gideon's only reply was to close his eyes, nod his head back, and snore theatrically.

"You two are a lost cause." He turned back to Tim. "You're absolutely right. Multiple observers increase the effect exponentially. Now, remember that we, our bodies and brains and even memories, are also matter and energy. If a willworker were to remove themselves completely from our society, stop weaving, and live solely in the normal world, what would happen?"

A light came on in Tim's mind. "They'd forget, wouldn't they?"

"Exactly. Deniers eventually forget everything, but

sadly the craving for the rush of manipulating the elements remains. Imagine what it would be like to be addicted to something but not remember what it is, not remember when or where you experienced it, not even consciously remember what it felt like. Deniers tend to suffer from all kinds of emotional and mental problems: depression, anxiety, paranoia, even insanity and suicide."

"Wait, what?!" said Tim, almost angrily. His mind was suddenly whirring like a top. "But why? Why would anyone become a Denier?"

"Why do people ever do stupid things? Love and loss, usually." Kieran sighed and shifted in his chair. "Someone they care about dies, or they experience something truly horrible. Or worse, they fall in love with a Sleeper and choose to be with them instead."

"They risk insanity for someone they love," said Tim softly, almost to himself. His heart was hammering in his chest. Was it possible? He suddenly got up and walked away from the fire. It was too huge of an idea for him to sit still.

"Hey," called Gideon, getting up from his loveseat, "you're not having another freakout, are you?"

"Freakout?" asked Kieran.

"He had a panic attack earlier," explained Vee. She got up too and followed Tim. "Hey, are you okay?"

"No, I'm fine, I'm just..." What was he? Excited? Scared? He turned suddenly back to Kieran. "Can they come back? Deniers, what happens if they try to come back?"

"They rarely do. Sometimes, with younger people, they will leave over some drama and come back in a month or two, but the longer they are away, the harder it becomes. The mind builds up walls to keep the magic out. Breaking the walls, well," —he sighed— "sometimes the cure is worse than the disease."

"But if they get over it, the breaking of the walls or whatever, do they get better?" Tim was talking faster and faster now. "If they go crazy from forgetting, can coming back cure them?"

Kieran frowned. "That's a very specific question. What are you getting at?"

"I think…" Tim took a big breath. "I think my dad is a Denier."

"No," Kieran immediately shook his head. "Impossible."

"But you just said…"

"I said people in your family tree, an ancestor on each side. Something like that. For a Denier to have a child who has the gift is almost mathematically impossible."

"Almost?" Tim grabbed at the word. "Then it could happen?"

"One in a million chance. It's a double-recessive gene, remember? The odds of a Denier meeting and marrying someone who carries both? Astronomical."

"But you said before that people who carry it are drawn to each other!" He was almost yelling now.

"Tim," Kieran cut in, "why are you so hung up on this?"

"*Because it would explain everything!!*" For a moment everyone stared at him, and he realized how loud he had gotten. "I'm sorry, I just…" He thrust his hands into his hair and turned away. "It would explain so much."

"Tim." Vee walked up and hesitantly put a hand on

his left arm, turning him back to her. "What's wrong? What's up with your dad?"

Tim dropped his arms to his sides and looked at each of his companions. Could he do it? Could he actually tell them? He swallowed, then took a deep breath and closed his eyes.

"My father…has schizophrenia. He's in a hospital, maybe forever. He went there on his own because…" Without opening his eyes, Tim raised his scarred left hand. "Because of this."

"*Oh,*" said Vee in a barely audible voice. She covered her mouth with her hands. Gideon sat down suddenly on the arm of his loveseat, his face blank and stunned. Kieran sat motionless, his brow furrowed as if he were still trying to make sense of what he'd heard. He was the first to break the silence.

"How old were you?"

"No, Kieran," Vee interrupted, "just leave him, he doesn't…" She turned back to Tim. "Oh god, the panic attack, you thought you were…oh, Tim, I'm so sorry, I didn't know, we didn't mean to push you so hard." She looked like she was on the verge of tears.

"No, stop." Tim looked at them at last. Sympathy he expected, but something about the stunned horror of his new friends touched something inside him. "It's okay, Vee, there's no way you could have known. I'm okay. Really." He smiled at her, then looked directly at Gideon, then at Kieran. "I want to. I want to talk about it." He was surprised at the truth of his own words. He walked back to his chair and sat, elbows on knees, and examined his left hand in the firelight.

"I was seven," he began.

Chapter 12

Timmy Hansen is seven years old. He has red-blonde hair like his daddy and gray eyes like his mommy, and he lives in the big brown house on Elm Street. That's just how he says it when Mrs. Rainn calls on him in class, the big brown house at 1402 Elm Street. He loves his house, with its creaky old floors and three stairways and rooms rooms rooms to explore on rainy days. He is an only child, another thing he announces with pride, and the house is much too big for the three of them, but Timmy likes it just fine.

He doesn't understand what his mommy's job is, something to do with selling houses, but his daddy is a teacher and a writer. The best times are when Daddy gets "on a roll", because then he takes time off from his job at the big college and spends lots of time at home. Daddy calls it a big word that sounds like "bat-call", but Timmy knows that isn't right. What he does know is that Daddy spends hours on the couch with his laptop, typing away or flipping through pages in a big binder, making notes with a red pen. If he's mousy-quiet, Daddy will let him cuddle up next to him while he works, and that's one of his favorite things, wrapping up in a blanket, leaning back against Daddy, smelling his Daddy-smell of coffee and aftershave, while he tap-taps or scritch-scratches away. He plays on his DS with the sound off or colors a picture or even writes his own stories sometimes. This is hard because Timmy doesn't always know the right words or how to spell them, but it always makes Daddy super happy when he tries.

But Daddy hasn't been very happy lately, or writing very much, but he has been home more. Much more. Sometimes he hears Mommy and Daddy talking or even arguing late at night when he's supposed to be asleep. He hears the word "medication" a lot, which he knows means medicine, but Daddy hasn't been sick, just sad and sometimes angry or scared. More and more Daddy says No when Timmy wants to play, and more and more the smell from him isn't coffee but something that smells like sour smoke, and the drink on the table is a glass with ice and a brown grown-up drink instead of a coffee mug more often than not.

Timmy doesn't really understand all of this, so one day he asks Mommy if Daddy is sick, and Mommy's eyes get all crumply like she is going to cry.

"Oh, honey, listen, Daddy isn't sick, not like that. He just has some problems and has to stay home from work for a while." She hugs him tight and he notices she feels bonier, harder than she used to.

That night, Mommy and Daddy have their biggest fight ever, with yelling and crying from both of them, but after that, things get better. The glasses turn back into coffee mugs, and Daddy smiles again, but he doesn't write at all anymore. Instead, he takes long naps on the couch or stares out the window daydreaming. Sometimes he will jump a little when he does this, like he fell asleep and then woke up, and whenever he catches Timmy watching him, he always gives a brave smile, like he's doing something hard and he's proud of himself.

Then the letter comes.

Timmy is playing upstairs when it arrives, and the first he knows about it is a sound like a bomb going off downstairs. He sneaks down and sees Daddy in a rage, throwing things in the kitchen while Mommy sits sobbing in a chair, a piece of paper dangling from one hand. Timmy doesn't let them see him. He just goes back up as quickly as he can and hides under the blankets with a pillow over his head to drown out the noises. After a long time, he hears a muffled voice.

"Timothy?"

He peeks his head out and sees Daddy leaning against the doorframe looking sad and tired, but not mad.

"May I come in?"

Timmy nods and scoots up in the bed so Daddy has room, still hugging the blanket around himself like armor. Daddy sits and sighs.

"Did I scare you?"

Timmy nods.

"I'm so sorry." Daddy is quiet for a moment. "I want to tell you something. I think you're old enough to understand it now. Have you ever had a daydream so strong it seemed real?"

"All the time."

"And have you ever had a daydream that scared you?"

Timmy nods his head vigorously. "Like when the shadows at night look like monsters?"

"Just like that." Daddy takes a big breath before continuing. "Timothy, I have a problem where I can't control my daydreams. They seem as real as anything to me, and I can't make them stop."

Timmy's eyes grow wide at that thought. "It sounds really scary."

"It is, buddy. It really, really is. There are special medicines I can take that help, but they have side effects. That means that they help, but they do other things too. They make me very sleepy, which isn't bad, but they also make it so my imagination doesn't work right."

"But you need that to make your stories!" Daddy had told Timmy many times how writing worked. "How can you write your stories if you can't daydream them first?"

"Just so, and that is what I want to talk about with you. Mommy and I have decided that I should stop taking the medicine for a while to see if I can start writing again. I need to write because..." Daddy stops talking for a second and starts to look a bit angry. "Because the university just sent me a letter telling me they don't want me to teach there anymore."

"That's not fair! You really like teaching."

"Yes, I do, but it is very hard to teach when you have a problem like mine." Daddy smiles and reaches out to cup the side of Timmy's face. "Now I want to tell you something very important. When I stop taking my medicine, the problems with my daydreams will come back, probably worse than before. I might get scared or mad for no reason, but I want you to remember that no matter what, I would never do anything to hurt you, I promise."

"Okay." Timmy climbs over into Daddy's lap. He is happy, but a tiny seed of worry take root in his heart, even as Daddy hugs him.

For a couple of weeks, things seem to get back

almost to normal. Mommy is gone more because she has to sell more houses, but Daddy is writing again. He seems distracted sometimes, but he also seems happy. But as the weeks go by and Timmy starts second grade, things change. More and more, when Timmy comes home, he finds Daddy doing things other than writing: sleeping or watching TV or just pacing around his study. When he does write, he seems frustrated, and the trash can in the study is overflowing with crumpled papers.

One day he smells the sour-smoke drink smell on Daddy when he hugs him, though there is no glass on the table or in the sink. There are no more late-night arguments, but he hears Mommy and Daddy talking after bedtime, and their voices sound sharp and tense. For the first time in his young life, Timmy Hansen doesn't look forward to coming home after school.

Then comes the day when he wishes he'd stayed at school forever.

"Daddy?"

It's a gray, chilly, windy autumn day, and the first thing that Timmy notices that seems wrong is that there are no lights on in the house.

"Daddy? I'm home." He hangs his jacket (blue and black with a bright red monster on the back, Tim remembers it so clearly) *on the hook by the door and then wanders down the hall. Living room, kitchen, dining room all dark. I'm not scared, he thinks, I don't even need a nightlight anymore, so I'm not scared. But he jumps anyway when a particularly strong gust makes the old house shift and groan slightly.*

"Daddy, where are you?" A little bird of panic starts to flutter in his chest, but then he hears muttering

and papers moving around in the back of the house. Relieved, he runs through the dining room and checks Daddy's study.

The room is a mess, with papers strewn everywhere, books pulled down off shelves, and desk drawers open, overflowing with disturbed contents. Daddy is sitting on the floor by the window, searching desperately through a wastepaper basket between his knees, tossing crumpled papers and old tissues over his shoulder like a dog digging for a bone, all the while muttering under his breath. Timmy steps into the room and Daddy jumps so dramatically that Timmy almost starts giggling, but the laughter dies when he sees the look of real fear on Daddy's face.

"OH! God!" He takes several deep breaths, closes his eyes and shakes his head like he's trying to wake himself up. "Timothy. I didn't hear you come home, buddy."

"I yelled 'I'm home', didn't you hear me?"

"No, I...I guess I was busy." Daddy looks around the room as if seeing the mess for the first time.

"How come there's no lights on, Daddy? It's a really gloomy day."

"The power's out. Wind must have knocked down some branches, taken out the lines." The confused look fades from Daddy's face. "I was looking for a flashlight. That's why I didn't hear you, I was busy looking."

"In the trash can? That's silly, Daddy."

"You're right, it is." Daddy smiles, but just a little one, like he's worried. Then he gets up onto his knees and holds out his arms. "Loving?"

Timmy doesn't need a second invitation. He backs

up three steps, then runs and leaps into Daddy's arms as hard as he can, toes scrabbling for purchase as he dangles from Daddy's neck.

"Knock! You! Over!" says Timmy through gritted teeth.

"No, no, no, nononononoAHHHHH!!" With exaggerated crashing sound effects, Daddy tumbles onto his back with Timmy on top, giggling like mad. It is their daily ritual, and it never gets old.

"Love you, Daddy, you're silly."

"And I love you. Now up, you're squishing me." This only makes Timmy squirm around and bounce more, producing more silly sound effects from Daddy. This, too, is part of the ritual.

"Ugh. Uhh. Ugh. Ah. Okay, okay, enough already!" With a laugh, he hugs Timmy tight. "So, it probably will get chilly in here with the power off. Want some hot cocoa?"

"Yessss! With marshmallows? And can we do candles?"

"Candles and cocoa it is."

Fifteen minutes later, Timmy is sitting at the dining room table, sipping a large mug of cocoa with marshmallows. Daddy has found a pair of big silver candlesticks and tall candles to go in them, so the table seems very fancy, an island of soft light in the gloom. Daddy was right, the house is getting colder, so Timmy has grabbed one of his blankets from his bed and wrapped himself up in it. The house continues to creak and moan at every gust, but while Timmy is getting used to the strange noises, Daddy jumps at every sound.

"It's just the wind, Daddy," says Timmy after the fifth time.

"Yes, I know!" he snaps, then sighs and looks sorry. "I know. I've just never liked days like these. The wind, it sounds like something is trying to scratch its way in. Something..." He stops and shudders. "Never mind." He picks up his own mug and stalks out of the dining room. Timmy hears him clinking around for a few minutes, then Daddy comes back carrying a brown bottle, which he sets on the table. Another strong gust buffets the house and Daddy recoils away from the windows, his upper lip pulled back from his teeth in a fear-filled snarl. He relaxes as the wind fades. He takes another gulp from his drink, still staring out the window.

"I can hear them. I've always been able to hear them." He looks at Timmy and his eyes are too bright, too wide, too shiny. He sets his mug back on the table and crouches down next to Timmy. "The things *in the air. They pretend to be birds sometimes, but they're not."*

"Daddy, you're scaring me."

"No!" Daddy looks seriously shocked at this. "No, Timothy, listen. I'm not telling you this to scare you." He reaches out and cups Timmy's face. "I never want you to be scared. I want you to be safe. I will always *keep you safe, even when you're as big as me." He kisses Timmy on the forehead. "But you deserve to know..."*

Then the strongest gust yet hits the house, and a loud CRASH comes from the living room. Daddy springs up and turns, putting himself between Timmy and the sound, but as he turns his arm catches the bottle on the table, dumping its contents. The whiskey spills across the tablecloth and onto Timmy, soaking his entire left side, especially the sleeve of his shirt. A cold breeze blows through the room, causing the candles to gutter (but not go out).

"NO!" Daddy bellows, making Timmy jump. "GET OUT OF MY HOUSE! STAY AWAY FROM MY FAMILY!" *He flails his arms around, striking out at an unseen enemy. Timmy huddles in his chair, terrified, no longer aware of the cold liquid or the fumes that are making his eyes water.* "You'll not have them! Get out! Get…"

Daddy swings an arm out and hits one of the candlesticks, knocking it loose from the holder. It tumbles, and lands in the whiskey puddle. The flames pour across the table like a second spill of liquid, and Timmy cannot get away. Out of pure instinct, he brings his hand up to block his face.

Then there is light and heat and pain and screams.

****

"It was an accident," said Tim softly. He sniffed, and suddenly realized his cheeks were wet with tears. He scrubbed at them with the heel of his hand, embarrassed. "He was trying to protect me from whatever he was seeing. But the next thing I remember, it was two weeks later, I was in the hospital, and he'd checked himself into an institution. He's been there ever since, just…getting worse."

He looked up at his new friends. Kieran was watching him with complete attention, Gideon was staring into the fire, Vee was back in her circular chair, curled up on her side, her face hidden in shadow except for the reflection of the firelight in her eyes.

"How long were you in the hospital?" Kieran asked.

"About six weeks. My mom came home just as it happened, otherwise I probably would have died and the house would have burned down. As it was," —he smiled ruefully— "it wasn't the burns, it was the infections afterward that kept me in. The grafts wouldn't take right, I almost lost my hand, and I had to do physical therapy for years to get the full range of movement back." He rubbed the back of his hand. "I don't have much feeling in it either."

"Is that why you do that flexing thing?" Gideon held up his own hand and moved it back, forth, side, side.

"Yeah, it's a nervous habit now." Tim fell silent. He felt wiped out like he'd just run a 5K. Now that he'd finished, he really didn't know what would happen. Suddenly, Vee stood up and walked over to him, the light behind her obscuring her face. She stopped in front of him and held out her hands. Tim hesitated for a moment before accepting them, and with a gentle tug, she pulled him up to his feet. As he stood, the light shifted on her face, and he noticed the tracks of tears on her cheeks. She looked up at him, smiled, and threw her arms around his neck.

"Bravest. Thing. Ever," she whispered in his ear.

A knot of tension Tim hadn't realized was even there seemed to loosen inside his chest. He hugged her back tightly, lifting her off her feet, which made her giggle. Tim found himself laughing too, and he swung her around in a circle. He looked over and saw Gideon standing up, grinning. He walked over, threw his massive arms around both of them, picked them up and started flailing them from side to side like rag dolls.

"WhoooAH-OH-oooOH!" Tim cried out through

his now-hysterical laughter.

"Crushing…me…big…oaf!"

Gideon laughed and dropped them, breathless and disheveled, back to the floor. As they caught their breath, Tim noticed that Kieran was ignoring them completely, just staring into the fire, fingers steepled together. Vee noticed too, and walked over to the older Dusker.

"Wassup, Redbeard? Why are you ignoring us goofy teenagers?"

"I think," he said after a moment, and he turned and looked at Tim, "there's a chance you might be right about your dad."

Chapter 13

"Wait, what?" Tim came around to stand between Kieran and the fireplace. "You just said that it was impossible."

"No, I said it was a one-in-a-million chance."

"You did say impossible," piped up Vee.

"She's right," came Gideon's voice from the shadows.

"*In any case,*" Kieran cut in, looking annoyed, "some of the things you said about your father made me think that maybe, *maybe* there's a chance he's a Denier." He looked at Tim. "How old is your dad?"

"Umm, thirty-seven. He'll be thirty-eight in March."

"So that would have made him, what, thirty or so when the accident happened?" Tim nodded. Kieran chewed on his lip for a moment before continuing. "From the way you described things, it sounded like his schizophrenia was something new then. Am I right?"

Tim thought hard about this. "I think so, from what I remember. I was young. Is that important?"

"It might be." Kieran stood up suddenly and headed toward the shelves of books, still talking as though he assumed the others would follow. "I've studied psychology, so I know a bit about schizophrenia. It tends to start young, usually in the teens, sometimes younger than that. For someone to first show signs of it in their thirties is unusual."

They wound their way deeper into the stacks to the back wall, aetherlights flickering to life as they approached. The books there were massive, dusty tomes, bound in fading green leather with writing on their spines that seemed to dance and flicker when Tim wasn't looking directly at them.

"What are these, K?" asked Gideon.

"Genealogies." Kieran knelt and started running his hands over the spines on the bottommost shelf, muttering under his breath. He then gave a snort of satisfaction and pulled out a volume the size of an atlas. He stood with effort and turned to Tim.

"This is going to take some time."

"No kidding." Tim eyed the monstrosity in Kieran's arms.

"We Opacaroi keep detailed genealogical records." He shouldered past Tim and the twins and headed back toward the fire. "But when someone becomes a Denier they are expunged magically from the traditional rolls."

"But if my dad is a Denier, what good is looking at those books going to do then?"

"Ah." Kieran set the tome down with a thud next to the scones and tea. "That's the thing. Magical removal leaves traces, inconsistencies, problems in the texts both before and after. That's what I need to search for. The newer records are kept in Avalon, but the older volumes are sent here for safekeeping. If I can find errors in these old family trees, then I should be able to trace the lineage back to the modern day."

"Kieran, you don't have to—"

"Yes, I do, but listen to me." He fixed Tim with a sober gaze and held one hand out over the book. "I may find nothing. Your father may be a normal guy with a mental illness and this may be a complete waste of time. But if he is a Denier, that may be worse."

"How?"

"With what you describe, the state he's in, exposing him to anything having to do with Duskers may damage his mind further. He may go deeper into his psychosis, have a psychotic break, perhaps even fall into catatonia. But," —and here he smiled— "you deserve to know the truth. Just promise me that if he is a Denier, you won't do anything rash, alright?"

Tim thought about Forestview, about Watterman, and about the decision facing his mom. "Alright, just find out what you can, okay?"

"I will. You deserve no less, my brave young friend." Kieran extended his hand. Tim took it gratefully, and was surprised when the older man grinned and pulled him into a hug.

"Now, you should go." Kieran pulled away and placed his hands on Tim's shoulders. "I have work to do. Research, and…." He waggled a finger. "…preparations!"

"For what?"

"Whaddayathink, smart guy?" said Gideon from behind him. "Training, of course."

"Training…me?" Tim's stomach did a quick flip.

"No, the other incredibly gifted willworker we found last week." Vee's voice practically gushed sarcasm. "Yeah, you, ya dope. What, did you think it was all 'here's a whole new world of magic and monsters, have fun!' and then just toss you in?" She shook her pink-streaked mop and then sobered. "It's not a game, Tim. It's a war, the whole world is at stake, and we're losing. Maybe already lost. But we can't just give up, can we?"

"Do not go gentle into that good night," said Tim under his breath.

"Rage, rage against the dying of the light, precisely," Kieran finished.

"But yeah, K's right," said Gideon, standing and stretching, "we need to boogie before the Turning."

"The what?"

"Time's different here," Vee explained. "How long do you think we've been here, Tim?"

"Umm..." Tim thought about it and was completely flummoxed. It felt like almost no time had passed, like they'd just arrived, yet he knew he'd talked for a long time.

"Think that's a trip?" Gideon grinned. "Go feel your mug of tea."

Tim walked over and picked up his drink. Two-thirds of it was gone, but the remainder was just as piping-hot as it had been when Kieran gave it to him.

"That's impossible," he muttered.

"No," said Kieran, "that's time in the Duskrealms. It moves in fits and starts, moments staying suspended then hours popping by in a blink. It's always twilight here, always the between-time, but it occurs at dawn as well, not just dusk, and sometimes the shift from one to the other is rather jarring. We call those abrupt leaps forward a Turning, and once you spend some time here you will learn to feel when one's coming. There's one about to occur, and I think it would be best to get you back before it happens."

"Why? I don't understand."

"How do you think your mother would react if you

rolled home at six a.m. instead of dinnertime? When a Turning happens, the Duskrealms realign themselves with time in the normal world, stepping forward from dusk to pre-dawn or vice versa. Basically, we don't get you back through the waystones before the Turning occurs, you'll probably walk in on a freaked-out mother calling the police."

Tim pictured what would happen if he walked into the house at sunrise instead of while his mom was at the business dinner. Not pretty.

"Yeah," said Tim, "we should probably go."

As the four of them trudged back up the hill to the circle of stones, Tim's mind whirled with everything he'd experienced today. Had gym class really happened only 8 hours ago? He gazed up at the strange sky and felt a slight flutter of panic, but only slight, and laughed softly.

"What's so funny?" asked Vee.

"Nothing. Everything." Tim shook his head. "How do I go back?"

"Well, the waystones are much easier to use from here—"

"No, that's not what I meant." Tim laughed again. "Back to school. Back to homework and meatloaf and Dr. Who on Saturday nights." He looked back up at the moons. "It all seems so, I dunno, trivial now."

"The normal world isn't trivial," said Gideon. "That's what we're fighting for."

"Yeah, but whether I get an A on my algebra quiz really doesn't seem important anymore."

As they crested the hill and approached the ring of stones, Tim stopped. He felt something, a sort of tension in the air. It reminded him of the stillness that happens just before a summer thunderstorm. He turned in a circle, brows knitted together, trying to pinpoint the source of the feeling, and noticed Kieran watching him, arms crossed, a smile almost hidden behind his beard.

"You feel it already, don't you?" He nodded without waiting for a response. "It is too bad you can't stick around to watch the Turning. It's quite beautiful, once you get used to it."

"Used to it?"

"It's a little disconcerting the first few times." Kieran shrugged, then clapped his hands together. "Well, it's not like you're never coming back, is it? I will do what I can to look into the truth about your father, and next time you're here," —he grinned with anticipation— "no scones and tea for you, boy. We get to see what you can really do!" He stepped forward and embraced Tim, who stiffened only slightly. The closeness that seemed the norm among his new friends still felt odd, but he was warming to it faster than he thought possible.

Tim gestured toward the stones. "How do these things work?"

"Way easier than getting here," said Gideon.

"Lucky for you," muttered Vee half under her breath. Gideon shot her a look but she just looked up at the sky, whistling soundlessly.

"Anyway, I gotta go first so I can pick up the van. Just watch, and Vee will guide you home when it's your turn."

"What, will they just drop me off at my front door? Isn't that a little, I dunno, obvious?"

"No." Vee laughed. "The waystones can take you just about anyplace with a lot of nature, anywhere undisturbed. There's that stream that goes through the park a couple of blocks from your house, that'll do."

"Waitaminute." Tim gave the twins each a sharp look. "How do you know about Surrey Park?" They looked chagrined, but Kieran just rolled his eyes.

"Of course they know. They had to check on you before they made contact. Now go, Gideon, before the Turning starts!"

"Alright, alright!" Gideon walked up to the entrance to the circle, stopped, and took a deep breath. Tim felt something, like Gideon was about to draw, but he seemed to stay just on the edge, then a deep thrumming came from the stones. It wasn't a sound or something he felt, more like a sensation in his bones, the back of his neck, the soles of his feet. Gideon then walked through the nearest stone archway, but something strange happened. He seemed to *recede* from them, as if each step were taking him three strides away from them, then five, then ten, until he disappeared into a distance that wasn't actually there.

"Whoa."

"It's actually really easy," said Vee, stepping toward the stones, and then turned to face him. "Reach for the elements, but don't draw them. The stones will respond to that. Then close your eyes and picture your destination in your head, clear as you can, and you will feel it sort of lock into place. Then just start walking." She held out her hand, made a clumsy little curtsy, and batted her eyes. "May I escort you home, good sir?" She said it in a high, breathy, southern-belle voice, and Tim couldn't help but laugh.

"Why yes, young lady," Tim replied in a Foghorn Leghorn drawl, "you may, ah say, you may accompany me home."

"That was horrid." Vee scrunched up her face in disgust.

"Horrid?"

"Utterly."

"No worse than yours."

"I beg your pardon?"

"GO!" Kieran bellowed, and they both jumped. "Quit flirting and get him home before his mother calls out the hounds!"

"Okay, jeeze." Vee smiled at Tim and rolled her eyes. "C'mon, let's go." She reached out and took Tim's hand, and he tried very hard to convince himself that his heartbeat did not just speed up, or if it did, it was just nerves.

Tim closed his eyes and expanded his awareness outward, feeling the color/scent/feel of the elements, sensing Vee doing the same. The stones responded with the same deep, subaural sensation as before, but far stronger. As one, he and Vee stepped forward through the archway, accelerated forward, and disappeared.

****

As the youngsters left, Kieran ko Turian Aergead let his shoulders sag. There was so much even the twins did not yet know, and keeping up the positive appearance was exhausting. He trudged back down the hill, so lost in his thoughts that he hardly noticed when the heavenly bodies above him suddenly wheeled into new positions, phases of the moons all shifting slightly. The doors of Argent House opened without his gesture, recognizing their longest resident, leaving him to his musings.

The fireplace held nothing but embers now, and his

mug of tea was ice-cold, but a few logs on the former and a quick weave of Fire on both fixed that. Kieran slumped into the chair Tim had occupied during his long story and stared into the flames, rolling the mug slowly back and forth between his hands.

Who was Tim's father? A Denier or just some poor, sick man? Who was this new commander of the Midnighters? Tim's appearance so close to the disaster in the Southern Grottos was no coincidence, such things never were, and Tim's remarkable talent proved that, but what did it mean? And what of the issues his old friend Meneleas faced? He was well aware of the conflicts between Vee and her father, but he knew that if the twins had even an inkling of his real problems, they would be back in Avalon in an eyeblink, punishment be damned. Which, of course, would only make things worse.

He smiled slightly, a far different expression than any the teens had seen tonight. Three young people caught up in events way too big for them? Yes, that was a familiar scenario if there ever was one. Memories seemed to dance up out of the flames—he and Mel (no one called him that anymore, but he would always be Mel) and the other, the third, the one they never mention. The one *no one* ever mentions, at least by name. Betrayer, Corruptor, Forgotten One. Kieran shook his head. It was good that there could be no connection between Tim's father and the Betrayer. That would turn his old friend Mel's position from difficult to completely impossible.

Kieran laughed at his meanderings. Work to do now. He took a sip of tea and reached for the book of Opacaroi genealogy.

Chapter 14

Traveling to the Duskrealms had been like the world's worst carnival ride, but going back was a breeze. The only disorientation Tim felt was an odd instability with each step, as though he were walking along a series of ever-faster moving sidewalks. The sense of acceleration increased until he was sure his hair should be blowing back, only to stop abruptly. They both stumbled forward, and Vee lurched away with a curse and a splash. Tim opened his eyes.

He knew where they were almost as well as he knew his own bedroom; the culvert at the east end of Surrey Park, where a little unnamed stream passed under Linden Avenue before meandering into the subdivision and disappearing. Like any good introvert, Tim knew all the places of solitude within a mile of his house, and this was one of his favorites. He'd spent plenty of time here, hidden from the rest of the park by the hoary old willows and cattails, reading or daydreaming to the soothing sound of crickets and frogs.

Vee, however, did not seem charmed by their surroundings. She had pulled away from Tim because she had obviously come through above the water rather than on the bank. She was now sitting in the middle of the stream, soaking wet and so furious that Tim was surprised the water around her wasn't boiling. He bit his lips to hold back a guffaw of laughter.

The ear-splitting scream from behind him helped.

Startled, Tim jumped a foot and spun around. A guy and a girl, a few years older than them, lay on the bank just outside the culvert. Both were fumbling madly at their clothes and wore identical expressions of embarrassment morphing quickly toward anger.

"Oh," said Tim stupidly. "I…we didn't…umm, sorry, I…oh…we…"

"We didn't realize anyone else was here," cut in Vee with heroic aplomb. She had gotten to her feet while Tim was stammering and now walked over and took his hand. "Sorry, we'll go find somewhere else. C'mon, honey!" She dragged a still-mute Tim away from the couple. "Go back to what you were doing!" she called back over her shoulder.

The two of them climbed up the bank and into the park proper. Above, the remnants of sunset still lit the sky with soft purples, oranges, and pinks, and by the faint glow Tim could see that the park was already deserted. Despite what Kieran and the twins had told him, he was still floored.

"That's…incredible." He'd wanted to say "impossible" but found that word a little ridiculous. He turned to Vee and found her with both hands over her mouth, doubled over with silent laughter. "What's your malfunction?"

"You!" She burst into guffaws. "The couple…and you…oh goddess!" She wiped tears from the corners of her eyes. "I'm sorry, but you looked like a drowning fish!" And she went off again.

Tim eyed Vee and her dripping clothes up and down. "Better a drowning fish than a drowned rat!"

"Drowned rat!" Her laughter cut off. She glanced from side to side, then smiled evilly. "I'll show you a drowned rat, Hansen!" She raised her hands and wove Water. With a rushing sound, she pulled all the moisture out of her clothes and hurled it at Tim as a blinding mist. Tim wove a lattice of Air and Water between them and every droplet transformed into a snowflake. With a gesture, they swirled around him and coalesced into a snowball the size of a watermelon hovering between his outstretched hands. He looked at Vee and smiled innocently.

"Oh, you wouldn't dare!" She took a step backward.

Tim's smile broadened and, with a slight twitch of his fingers, he sent the massive snowball hurtling at Vee's head. Cat-quick, she ducked and it sailed off into the gloom.

"HA!" she crowed. "Did you really think an amateur move like that would work?"

"Nope," said Tim, still smiling. For a second, Vee looked confused, then her eyes widened. She tried to dive to one side, but FLUMP, the snowball, which had been hovering silently over her, collapsed onto her head.

"OHHHHH!" she screamed over Tim's laughter. "You are *so* dead!" With a wave, she gathered up the snow and launched a dozen projectiles at Tim. He tried in vain to block, parry, or sever her weaves, but between his laughter and her speed, he couldn't keep up. A snowball slipped past his guard and caught him full in the face, and he stumbled backward and fell on his back.

"Okay, okay, I give, I give!" He flung up his arms

to protect himself. Vee wove all the snow together again and stood over Tim threateningly.

"Do you yield?"

"Yes, yes, I yield!"

"Oh, that's no fun." She dropped the snowball and it dissolved into nothingness before even touching the ground. "You're supposed to be all defiant so I can pummel you into submission." She smiled, and for a moment he thought she was going to lie down beside him, but a buzz from Tim's pocket interrupted them. He dug out his phone.

"No." Seven texts from his mom. "Oh nononononono…" With a sinking feeling, he opened the texts.

—*6:42 Hey, dinner finished early. Want comida from anywhere?*—

—*6:47 No answer? Fine, I'll just get McDs*—

—*7:12 Still nothing, huh? QPwC and coke unless you say otherwise*—

—*7:26 WHERE ARE YOU?*—

—*7:34 There better be a good explanation for this, young man!*—

—*7:39 Your phone went straight to vm. Starting to freak. TEXT ME BACK*—

—*7:56 You have 15 minutes b4 I call the police.*—

It was now 8:03.

"What? What's wrong?" All playfulness had left Vee's voice.

"My mom, she's freaking out." Tim started typing.

—*Sorry sorry sorry!*—

—*WHERE ARE YOU?*—

—*Surry Park. Home in 5.*—

—*NOW.*—

"I gotta go. I'm in…I don't even know how much trouble I'm in."

"I understand." Vee held out her hands. He took them and she helped him to his feet. She kept hold of his hands and looked up at him, head cocked slightly to one side. "I meant what I said earlier."

"About what?"

"Bravest thing ever." She smiled and, before Tim could react, she went up on her tiptoes, kissed him on his scarred cheek, and stepped away. She chuckled at the stunned expression on his face.

"I'll be sure to tick off Mr. Hegler tomorrow so I can get Oh-Foured again. See you there?"

"Uhh, yeah."

"'Uhh, yeah?'" She shook her head, smile widening. "You need to work on your delivery, Hansen. Not very smooth." She waved and flounced off into the gloom.

Tim stood there for a full minute, his brain still trying to process what had happened when his phone buzzed again.

—*You now have 3 minutes.*—

"Crap," Tim muttered. He shook himself out of his stupor and took off at a run toward his house.

****

"Mom?" Tim tried to keep the dread out of his voice. It almost worked.

"Kitchen."

Tim swallowed and made his way down the hall. Anna was sitting at the breakfast nook, still in a gray business suit, her briefcase, phone, and a white carry-out bag on the table next to her. She looked calm, focused, and attentive, which Tim knew meant that she was mad enough to spit fire.

"Hi," said Tim lamely.

She said nothing. Tim swallowed again, his throat clicking.

"I'm sorry."

Still nothing.

"I tried to…"

"What's her name?"

"Wh-what?" His mom raised her eyebrows and stared at Tim for a beat before replying.

"You are a smart, shy, studious teenage boy. If a smart, shy, studious teenage boy suddenly starts acting stupid, there's usually a girl involved."

"Uhh…" Tim's mind was going a mile a minute. Did she really have an idea or was it just a guess? Anna extended her hand.

"Let me see your phone."

Tim dug it out of his pocket and handed it to her, confused. Was she looking for incriminating texts? She turned it over in her hands.

"Looks undamaged." She tapped at the screen. "Seems to be fully functional." She tapped some more and her own phone buzzed against the tabletop. "Certainly seems able to send text messages."

"Mom, I couldn't—"

"Which is the only reason," she cut across him, voice rising, "why my normally-thoughtful son would ever fail to contact me to see if he could go out after school, *which* I would have said no to since he had just finished a *detention for fighting*..."

"I'm sorry!"

"AND I WAS WORRIED SICK!" She got to her feet, eyes blazing. "What is happening with you? You disappear after this detention thing, I hear nothing, I have no idea where you've gone..."

"Mom..."

"...who you're with, if you've gotten into another fight..."

"Mom, please, listen..."

"...and then you waltz in all nonchalant..."

"Genevieve!"

Anna stopped dead, her mouth still open. "What?" The confusion on her face was almost comical.

"Her name...is Genevieve. But she hates it, so we call her Vee instead. *We* being me and her brother, Gideon. That's who I was with."

Anna sat back down slowly, shock, anger, confusion, and curiosity warring on her face.

"Vee." She said it slowly and carefully, as though tasting the name and not sure if she liked it or not. "So, a friend from school."

"Friends, she and Gideon both. They're...they're my friends." Tim was amazed at how right it sounded to say that.

"Are they in your classes?"

"No, they're older. I met them through Dan."

"Who's Dan?" He could hear the suspicion creep back into her voice. Internally, Tim slapped himself on the forehead. This wasn't going to make a very good impression.

"Daniel Lum. Dr. Lum. The guidance counselor?" *Here it comes...*

"So you blew off coming home after detention to go hang out with kids you met in the guidance counselor's office?" Despite the sharpness of her tone, Tim felt a sudden spasm of loyalty.

"Yes, mother, the same place I go every week, horrible miscreant that I am."

"Do *not* get cheeky with me, young man." She took a deep breath, brushed a strand of hair from her face, and crossed her arms in front of her. "Where did you go?"

"We went to their place." Tim knew he had to skirt the truth here. "They live on the other side of town, by the forest preserve. I met their...stepdad Kieran. Really nice guy, makes great scones."

"Scones?" She looked at Tim like he'd just proclaimed that he wanted to grow up to be a rodeo clown. "He makes scones?"

"Yeah, cranberry orange with lots of cinnamon."

"I thought you said you were at Surrey Park."

"We were," Tim said quickly. "We went to their place, then it was so nice and I wanted to be close to home so I—"

"So you could be sure to beat me home?" Anna sighed and shook her head. "Why didn't you just text me?" Her anger was gone, replaced with disappointment, which Tim thought was worse.

"I thought you'd say no, and I thought I had time. I put my phone in my bag and didn't hear it go off...I'm sorry, Mom. I didn't mean to freak you out."

"That's why you have the phone, Tim, so I don't freak out." She looked up at him for a moment, then smiled. "I can't stay mad at you. Just like your dad." She held up the bag. "C'mon, sit and eat. Unless you filled yourself up on scones, that is."

Tim grinned and joined her at the table, grabbing the bag and emptying the contents. She watched him as he unwrapped his burger and dug in, a tiny half-smile

135

playing at the corners of her mouth.

"What?" he mumbled around a mouthful of fries.

"Well?" Anna rolled her eyes innocently. "What's she like?"

"Mom! She's just a friend."

"Yah-huh", she said, blatantly unconvinced. "So, what's she like?

Tim huffed through his nose and popped another fry in his mouth, considering. "Six-and-a-half feet of enthusiasm in a five-foot package."

"So, definitely an opposites attract situation then, huh?"

"Mom, I told you—"

"She's just a friend, I heard." She took a sip of her own soda that had been sitting neglected on the table, leaving a ring of moisture there. "They're good people? I can trust you on that, right?"

Tim set his burger down and thought. *How much do I really tell her?* "When I got out of detention, the jock who got me in trouble was there with a couple of his friends." *Yeah, about a dozen of them.* "They were waiting for me." *They caught me under the bleachers and beat the snot out of me.* "Vee and Gideon, they stood up for me." *They used magical martial arts to beat the snot out of the jocks.* "If they hadn't been there, I don't know what would have happened." *I would have ended up in the hospital if not for them magically healing me.* "They're good people, Mom. The best." *They've recruited me to help save the world, and I think Dad was part of their group and went crazy because he stopped.* All the half-truths made Tim's stomach clench. He played with his fries, suddenly far less hungry.

Anna considered him for a moment, then smiled. "Fine, but this is the last time I will accept the I-forgot-to-text-you excuse. Are we clear?"

"Crystalline."

She stood up. "I'm going to go clean up. Do you have homework?"

Tim fixed her with his best are-you-serious stare.

"It wouldn't kill you to do some from time to time, you know."

"Yes, yes it would. I would die. Painfully." He went boneless in the chair, head to the side, tongue hanging out, and gurgled.

"Don't be smart." She swatted playfully at his lolling head. He dodged, and they smiled at each other.

"Love you, kiddo."

"Love you too, Mom."

Anna headed toward the stairs, then paused in the doorway.

"Genevieve and Gideon." She wrinkled up her face and shuddered theatrically. "People pick out the tackiest names for twins, don't they?"

"Yeah." Tim nodded. "I think that's half the reason Vee hates her name so much."

Anna chuckled and went up the stairs.

It wasn't until much later that Tim realized he had never told his mom that Vee and Gideon were twins.

Chapter 15

"You look like hell. Here."

Tim startled and almost put his elbow into his mystery meat. He'd been near-dozing at the cafeteria table, his lunch forgotten and cooling. He blinked twice and saw an enormous frozen coffee drink in front of him.

"Oh, my god, you're a saint." He took a huge slurp of chocolate-coffee goodness and looked up at last. Vee and Gideon were sitting with him, both with coffee drinks of their own and looking just as exhausted.

"I know why I'm wiped out. What's your excuse?" Tim took another long pull at his drink.

"Going back and forth to the 'Realms screws up your internal clock," said Gideon between his own sips. "I know I didn't sleep for crap last night, so I figured you'd need one of these bad boys too."

"Easy there, tiger," said Vee. "You go too fast and you'll end up with a..."

"Owwwww!!!" Tim pressed a hand to his forehead and whimpered.

"...brain freeze," she finished with a sympathetic smile. "Well, it wasn't just cosmic jet lag that kept me up."

"Okay, what?"

"Same as you, dummy!" She smacked him playfully on the shoulder. "Now that we found you, we won't have to worry about this crap anymore." She gestured vaguely around them. "We can concentrate on the important stuff."

"Yeah, of course." Tim took another small sip and tried to squash the little worm of disappointment he felt. "I wish I had that option."

"What do you mean?"

"Well, maybe you guys can go back to Avalon full-time, but I can't. Kinda have those parental expectations I have to fulfill."

"Yeah," said Vee softly. "I know what those are like."

"What do you..." Tim's question trailed away as his ears caught the click-tap-click-tap of crutches, and a knot of crew cuts and football jerseys approached the table.

"Well, if it isn't Freakshow and his little bodyguards."

"Piss off, Petersen," drawled Gideon. "We ain't in the mood. Or did you already forget how things went yesterday?" A couple of the jocks suddenly looked nervous.

"Temper, temper," Kyle continued without missing a beat. "We're just having a little chat. Aren't we, Freakshow?"

Tim had to suppress an almost-overwhelming urge to throw his drink in Kyle's face. "I have zero interest in anything you have to say, Hop-a-Long." To his annoyance, Petersen's smile only got larger, and there was something odd about his eyes.

"Oh, you should. Really. Because it would break my *heart*," —he put an odd emphasis on the word and his gaze flickered to Vee— "if we didn't pay the three of you back for your…hospitality. That kind of rudeness doesn't run in my *blood,*" his gaze flicked to Gideon, then back to Tim. "See you around." He turned and started click-tapping away.

It was too much for Tim. He drew and wove Air.

"No, Tim, *don't!*" Vee said in a horrified stage whisper.

It felt like Tim's brain was running full tilt and slammed into an invisible metal wall. One with spikes. Rusty ones.

"Oh…god…" The pain was so huge he couldn't even cry out. He doubled over and grabbed his head in his hands, hoping to keep it from blowing itself to pieces.

"Yeah, we probably should have warned him about that," said Gideon softly. "You gonna live, dude?"

"No," croaked Tim. "What happened?"

"You just got a crash course in the Unbelieving." Vee scooted closer to Tim and gently rubbed his back. "Remember what Kieran talked about yesterday? All that quantum stuff?"

"Yeah?" Tim raised his head ever so slowly.

"Well, you just tried to make a gust of wind appear inside a building, pick up an obnoxious jock, and fling him across the room. But you did it in front of three hundred or so people who believe that it's impossible for that to happen. That's the Unbelieving. Kieran calls it 'the calcification of reality'. If you try to do something too blatantly magickal, the unbelief of the people around you shuts it down and you with it."

"It's like a tug of war between a bodybuilder and three hundred kindergarteners," said Gideon. "Doesn't matter how strong he is, he's gonna lose."

"But if I'd tried it in front of just a couple of people…"

Vee was already shaking her head. "Doesn't work like that. Even just one Sleeper is enough. It's like you're not just fighting through every belief they have, but the belief of everyone they know, everyone they've ever had contact with."

"But how come it worked in the park last night?" Tim massaged his temples. The pain was fading but his brain felt bruised.

"The park was deserted, remember? Under those circumstances it will work if you're careful. If you're not…"

"You end up with a Texas-sized headache." Tim sniffed and blinked a few times. "But I've seen you do stuff in front of Sleepers. The lights in Oh-Four, the martial arts stuff?"

"Coincidental," said Gideon. "It's possible for lights to flicker or for a couple of teenagers to know kung fu, and it's possible for a jock running the mile to trip over his own feet."

"Or get tripped by someone else." Vee shrugged. "So if you can explain it away, you can do it. If not, then migraine city."

"I suppose that explains why Duskers don't rule the world." Tim sniffed again and took a tentative sip of his drink. The cold felt amazing but the last thing he needed right now was another brain freeze.

"Exactly." Vee's expression suddenly changed, first concerned then mildly amused. "You, umm, you gave yourself a nosebleed."

"What?" Tim touched his nose and felt wetness. He looked at his fingers, saw the bright smear of crimson, and swore. He turned to his tray for a napkin, but in his stupor he had forgotten to grab one.

"Don't freak, I've got some tissues." Vee dug around in the front of her massive purple backpack and pulled out a packet. "Here, let me help." She reached toward Tim's face.

Instinctively, Tim flinched away. Vee froze, her hands outstretched, the small smile on her face fading.

"Fine," she said flatly and dropped the packet on the table. "I guess it's still 'touch bad', huh?" She stood up. "Clean yourself up then. I gotta go."

"Vee, wait, I—"

"I gotta go!" She slung her bag up over her shoulder so hard that she stumbled, then stalked off. Tim gaped after her for a moment, then turned to Gideon who shrugged.

"Hey, we share some genes, doesn't mean I understand her." He reached over and snagged an apple off Tim's tray. "But she's right, we gotta bounce. See you after school?"

"Umm, yeah." Tim absently grabbed the tissues and dabbed at his nose. Gideon looked at him and winced.

"Yeah, you might wanna go clean up before class. You look like you got mugged, dude. Later." Tim waved, gathered up his things as best he could with one hand, and headed for the nearest bathroom.

Once he got a look in the mirror, he saw what the fuss was about. He had a rust-colored smear from nose to his cheekbone. He grabbed some paper towels, wet them, and dabbed at his face.

"Clean yourself up all you want, you'll still be ugly, Freakshow."

Tim whirled toward the voice, his head giving a final, faint throb. The door to the last stall swung slowly open and Kyle Peterson walked out, hands in his pockets, smiling slightly.

"Oh, what the hell do you want?" Tim was surprised at how unafraid he felt. Normally, if he was alone in the bathroom and Mr. Most Likely walked out of a stall he would...

Walked.

"You unbelievable pusswad. You faked your ankle being hurt, didn't you!"

"Oh no." Kyle looked down at his bandaged foot and flexed it. "It hurts like hell. I just don't care. And I really don't need to pretend around you, do I?" He giggled, a high, creepy sound that just didn't seem right for him. Suddenly Tim felt a sharp, unpleasant shiver. It wasn't the same as from weaving, more like when someone ran their fingernails down a chalkboard or rubbed two pieces of Styrofoam together, and then the lights in the bathroom faded. Not went out, but dimmed like a cloud passing over the sun.

"What the hell?"

"Mmm, appropriate, Dusker whelp. How's your head, by the way?" Kyle walked slowly toward Tim, his smile growing, and in the dim light he finally noticed what was wrong with the jock's eyes; either they had turned from blue to black or they were so dilated that no iris was left.

All the stories are true. Kieran's words echoed in Tim's mind. He didn't know what this thing in front of him was, but he did know one thing.

No worries about headaches.

Tim wove Air into a wall and blasted it at the Kyle-thing. Immediately he felt that same unpleasant prickle and his attack began to weaken. Instead of knocking it through the back wall of the bathroom, it only stumbled backward, looking surprised and annoyed.

It can sever weavings, Tim thought, his stomach turning cold. The Kyle-thing gestured and the shadows in every corner and under every surface seemed to come alive, twisting into a dozen black tentacles that slithered toward Tim from every side.

"You wanna play rough, whelp?" The Kyle-thing was grinning again. "We can play rough," and the tentacles whipped toward him.

Tim wove instinctively, and a pair of blue-and-scarlet blades appeared in his hands. He hacked and spun, desperately trying to create some space around him. Wherever his weapons met shadows, there was a hiss like water on a hotplate and the black tentacle would retract, but Tim was no fighter, no trained Dusker. One snuck under his guard and hooked an ankle, spilling him over backward, jarring his already tender head. The blades evaporated into floating embers, and eight more shadows darted in, twining around his arms and legs. The Kyle-thing advanced, grinning, but then another memory popped into Tim's head, as clear as someone whispering it into his ear.

It's easiest when you have an obvious source.

God, I'm a dolt, he thought, and he wove, hard.

Every tap in the bathroom erupted, the water forming into dozens of fists that dove at the Kyle-thing. Now it was the one fending off attacks from all sides, stumbling backward. Tim saw an opening, coalesced all the water together, and threw everything at it. A massive geyser of water slammed into the Kyle-thing's chest, and hurled it into the wall hard enough to knock dust loose from the ceiling. The shadow tentacles immediately vanished, but Tim took no chances. Weaving Air and Earth with the water, he formed a cage of ice around the Kyle-thing, trapping it. For a heartbeat, Tim stared at his handiwork, then bolted.

****

After a count of sixty, the *vrolach* opened Kyle's eyes. That had gone fairly well, it thought, though the whelp was freakishly strong. It drew in Darkness then lashed out, and Tim's ice cage vaporized. It stood up, then used another Darkness weave to push the wetness out of Kyle's clothes. *No need to go around dripping,* it thought, and giggled. It was aware of a new pain in this body's back, but it cared no more for that than for the ankle. The gibbering of Kyle's mind peaked as spasms rippled up and down the body's spine, then faded. The boy's consciousness was cracking quicker than the *vrolach* had hoped. If it stayed much longer, he'd end up a vegetable, no fun there. Good thing it should only need the meatsuit for a few more hours. It heard the first period bell ring.

"Time to check in," it muttered. It spied Tim's coffee drink, forgotten on the sink, took a swig, tossed the rest into the garbage, grabbed Kyle's crutches, and headed for the door.

It made its way upstairs, going slow and clumsy to keep up appearances, past the stragglers hustling off to class, and approached the offices in the rotunda. It paused at a door, frustration and fear warring on Kyle's face for a moment, then knocked.

"Enter," said a voice on the other side.

The *vrolach* opened the door, stepped inside, and

approached the desk deferentially.

"It is done, Master."

"Excellent. And the boy?"

"Frightened, but unharmed, as you ordered, though I do not understand—"

"You don't need to understand, darkspawn. Just obey."

"Yes, Master." The *vrolach* bowed, but scowled slightly.

"Now, I have a new task for you, one you should enjoy quite a bit. I have more of your ilk on retainer, so to speak, and they need cozy homes like yours. I just need you to gather up more of Mr. Peterson's friends and bring them here one at a time."

The *vrolach* smiled; he knew what this meant. "I look forward to the chance to peel the skin off the scar-faced one, Master. He…ukk…"

It fell to its knees, gagging like a cat with a hairball, and darkness seeped from its eyes and ears. The man behind the desk gazed at this scene, nonplussed except that his eyes were now glowing red-black.

"You're thinking again," he said calmly. "I did not bind you so that you could think, you arrogant little Murk. I bound you so that you could be my cat's-paw and do the dirty deeds I don't feel like bothering with myself." The light went out in his eyes and the Kyle-thing collapsed, gasping for air. "Go. Find jocks. Bring them here. Very simple. And if I catch you thinking for yourself again, I will shred you like tissue paper."

The *vrolach* staggered to its feet. "Y-yes, Master." Without looking up, it reached behind it, fumbled the door open, and left.

The man behind the desk rubbed his face, his shoulders sagging. He'd hardly slept in the last three days, between the preparations, the rituals, and raw nerves. Fifteen years of planning, and it all came down to the next 12 hours or so, and the behavior of three teenagers. He'd studied Meneleas' twins for over a year, and he had a good feel for how they'd behave, but the wild card was Tim. Was he his father's son, or his mother's? Everything hinged on that.

The Midnighter let out a sigh and started rummaging in one of the drawers of his desk. It would take time for the *vrolach* to bring anyone, so he should unwind as best as he could. He brought out a flat, black box, opened it, took out three professional throwing darts., and held them up to the light, examining them closely.

"Tim, Gideon, and Vee," said Daniel Lum, "time to see if you fly true."

Chapter 16

Tim spent the next three hours terrified.

He passed from class to class as fast as he could without running, sure that some black-eyed *thing* was going to snatch him out of the crowd and drag him into some unused classroom. Every passing period he craned his neck to search the crowd for a flash of pink or blue-dyed hair, but no such luck. He spent each class clock-watching endlessly, both willing the hands to move faster and dreading another trek through the halls. All the while, the same questions kept running through his mind: would Vee get Oh-Foured? How mad was she? Why was she mad at all? Was she mad enough to blow him off? And what the hell would he do if he walked into the detention room and she wasn't there? He did have a bus pass, but he didn't know which would be worse, running into Kyle on the bus or while he was hoofing it home.

But despite his fears, 3:15 found Tim, very much unmolested, standing outside C-04 with his stomach in knots.

Please let her be there, or I'm toast.

Tim opened the door and let out a sigh of relief. There was Vee in all her punk-rock glory, picking at her fingernails and very pointedly ignoring him. He'd never been so happy to see someone so mad at him. He walked over to the table.

"Vee, we need to talk."

She kept picking.

"Okay, I know you're mad at me…"

"Mad?" She gave him a blatantly fake look of surprise. "Why would I be mad at you?"

"Well, you kinda stormed off after lunch."

"The world doesn't revolve around you, Tim Hansen. Did it ever occur to you that maybe I had somewhere to be? Or that maybe I was mad about something else? Did those possibilities ever cross your mind?"

"Okay…" Tim held up his hands. "I'm really confused."

Her facade of cheerfulness cracked a bit. "Glad I'm not the only one," she muttered, and went back to attacking her peeling polish. Tim opened his mouth, thought better of it, then went to sit down.

"I don't think so, Mr. Hansen." Mrs. Gibson looked at him archly over the top of her laptop. "You shall join me front and center this time." She gestured to the unoccupied table directly in front of her desk. He cast one annoyed look at Vee, and moved to the front of the class.

Detention crawled by. Tim tried to fiddle with some notes, read a book, even doodle a bit, but nothing helped. How could he explain anything to her when she was like this? He had to tell her about Kyle. She obviously must have felt him weaving during the fight, yet she didn't even ask him about it. He risked a couple of glances back at her, but each time she wouldn't meet his eye. When at last the bell rang, she bolted before he could even stand up from the table.

"Balls," he muttered, "now what am I gonna do?"

But to his surprise, Vee was waiting in the exact spot as yesterday, though with far less enthusiasm. He caught Mrs. Gibson smiling at them as she left.

"What?" She regarded him with just a hint of a smile. "Did you think I was gonna ditch you or something?

"Actually, yeah, I did."

She snorted. "Shows what you know. C'mon, Gids is waiting."

"Hang on. I gotta tell you something."

"Tell me in the van." She shouldered her backpack and started walking toward the stairwell. Tim jogged after her.

"Vee, just stop for a sec." She ignored him, so he grabbed her elbow. "Genevieve, *stop!*" She turned on him, snarling.

"Don't you *ever* tell me what to do!" A jolt of electricity shocked Tim's hand. He pulled away, wincing and shaking it. She turned away and started to push the door to the stairwell open, but he'd had enough. With a quick weave of Air, he slammed it shut in her face.

"Let go of the door, Tim," she said without turning.

"No." He felt her start to attack his weave, so he redoubled it, twisting the strands into ever more complicated patterns.

"Let go of the door, Tim." This time she said it through gritted teeth.

"Not until you listen to me."

"Fine!" She dropped her backpack and rounded on him. "What? What's so important that it couldn't wait until we were in the van, huh?!" Her words came faster. "You wanna talk about why I stormed off at lunch?

Fine, no problem! I was mad, okay?"

"No, Vee, that's not..."

She steamrolled over him. "I think I have a legitimate reason, I mean, somebody who you think is a friend, who you think trusts you, suddenly he acts like you have some kind of disease or something."

"Umm, you should—" Tim started backing up, his gaze flicking to a point over her shoulder.

"That hurts, and maybe I overreacted a little, got snippy, but that's me, okay, you know that, and I know you have your issues, I get that, but I thought maybe, I dunno, you were getting past that and OH MY GODDESS YOU'RE NOT EVEN LISTENING TO ME, ARE YOU?!?"

Tim didn't even flinch at her final outburst. He was too busy staring past her, his face set and pale.

"Vee," he said evenly, "turn around."

She did. Standing behind her was what looked to be half of the football team. They had come down the stairs and through the door during her tirade, and now stood spread out between them and their easiest exit route, identical smiles on each of their faces. One of them was rummaging idly through Vee's backpack.

"Aww," said Kyle, standing in the very center of the group, "we interrupted a little lover's spat. How revolting."

Vee smirked and started weaving something. "Oh, you picked the wrong day to do this, Kyle."

"I don't think so." He gestured vaguely. Tim felt that same crawling sensation, and Vee's weave fell apart.

"Oh no," she whispered, and backed up until she bumped into Tim, who now saw that every one of the figures before them shared Kyle's iris-less eyes.

"Oh yes." The Kyle-thing grinned. "Genevieve no Seriah Corvitae, I think this fight is going to go a little differently than our last one." As one, the jocks started forward.

Whip-crack fast, Tim lashed out with a weave of Water and Fire, directed not at the *vrolachi*-possessed boys but at the pipes above them. One burst, showering the jocks with scalding mist and steam, and they recoiled, growling like animals.

"*Run!*" He grabbed Vee's hand and they bolted toward The Pit, the thunder of a dozen pairs of feet behind them.

"Do what I do," Vee yelled as they ran. She began weaving some strange mix of Spirit, Fire, and Air. Tim copied her, and felt the weave sink into his muscles just as four figures stepped out of the shadows ahead of them. Literally. They stepped *through* the shadows as though they were doorways, magically appearing behind pillars and posts. The lead one, a big blocky boy with a crew cut, made to grab at Tim. Everything seemed to slow down, and Tim ducked easily under, grabbed a wrist, pivoted, and flung his attacker twenty feet into the mob behind them. He stared at his hands.

"Wow," he whispered.

"No time!" Vee jumped in the air and kicked two different attackers. A fourth tried to come around her blind side, but Tim stomped a foot, wove Earth, and a shockwave rippled out and knocked the *vrolach* off his feet. Vee wove Air, and Tim instinctively ducked. Her purple monstrosity of a backpack came flying past and hit the remaining attacker like a cannonball. In one smooth motion, she snapped it up off the ground, and they bolted for the stairwell.

As they pounded up the stairs two at a time, the lights flickered. They heard the door slam open below them.

"I hate *vrolachi!*" Vee panted.

"What the hell is a roll-locky?"

"*Vrolachi,*" she repeated. "Shadow demons. Not a good sign that there's so many of them. That means—"

She never finished her thought. The lights above them went out, and six black-eyed football players dropped on them from above. Tim threw one down the stairs, but the rest swarmed them, trying to cut off their escape. They grabbed Vee's arms and tried to pin her against the railing, but she jumped up, wrapped her legs around the neck of one attacker, and flipped him into the others. Tim jumped over the falling bodies and spotted another pipe on the ceiling, this one cold water. A quick weave snapped it and, mixing in Air and a bit of Earth into the spray, the stairs below them were instantly coated with ice.

"Nice one." Vee grinned. "That should buy us some time. C'mon, Gids can feel we're in trouble, let's go."

The door to the parking lot was in sight when the lights died, and they were swarmed from every direction. Their legs were kicked out from under them, fists and feet and shadow-limbs attacking from every side. Even weave-enhanced fighting skills are no good when you have two limbs to block six blows. Within seconds, Tim and Vee were pinned against the lockers, dangling a foot off the ground, their arms and legs bound by the same sort of shadow-tentacles Kyle had used in the bathroom. The Kyle-thing himself walked up to them, hands in his pockets, looking so pleased that Tim almost broke free trying to get at him.

"Temper, temper." The *vrolach* waggled a finger at Tim. "Now, that was a fun little game, wasn't it? And here I thought this was going to be hard, that I was going to have to go grab Mommy-dearest and use her as leverage. I'm almost disappointed."

"Leave my mother *alone!*" Tim tried to attack with a weave, but instantly it dissolved. But when they severed it, Tim felt something, something in the shadows that bound them...

"Let Tim go," said Vee in a commanding tone. "I know it's me you want. He's no threat to you or your master."

"Silly, arrogant girl, it's him my master wants, not you. Though the daughter of the First Speaker of Avalon does sweeten the pot a bit."

"Why do you want me?" Tim honestly didn't care, but he wanted to keep the thing talking. He kept probing gently at the shadows that bound them, and he felt something, something like a weave.

"If it were up to me, Freakshow, I would flay you alive and then strangle your little sweetheart here with your skin so you could watch her die first." A flicker of unease crossed the Kyle-thing's over-dilated eyes. "But it's not, and I don't ask questions."

"Hey, boys! Having a party without me? How rude!"

A large figure stood silhouetted against the afternoon sun. Gideon.

"Oh," the Kyle-thing smiled and started walking toward the doors, a half dozen teammates flanking him. "The party's just not the same without you."

"Tim, shut your eyes," Vee whispered. "Keep them shut and run for the doors as soon as you're free."

"I don't understand," Tim whispered back.

"Of course! And you know what every party needs, don't you?" Gideon seemed utterly unfazed by the situation. The *vrolachi* paused.

"Enlighten me," said the Kyle-thing.

Gideon burst out laughing. For a full ten seconds, everyone just stared at him as he nearly fell over with laughter. Finally, wiping his eyes with his left hand, he regained his composure.

"I absolutely cannot believe you just said that," he sniggered.

With one motion, Gideon pulled something from his right pocket, tossed it underhand, and ducked back, pulling his jacket up over his face. All the jocks scattered, and Tim saw a gray canister rolling along the floor, spitting smoke and sparks. He squeezed his eyes shut.

There was a *chuff,* then a thick, sputtering hiss, and the whole world lit up. Even through closed eyelids, Tim saw everything as a yellow-orange blur. The *vrolachi* all screamed, a high, grating sound like dry ice against metal, and Tim dropped to the floor. He ran, hunched over, eyes closed, his right hand running along the lockers, his left out in front, a thick, acrid stench in his nostrils. His hand met glass. He reached up, shoved on the push-bar, and stumbled out into the blessedly fresh air.

"Go, go, go!" Tim opened his eyes and saw Gideon's purple Bus pulled right up onto the grass. A brilliant white light streamed out of the doors, like a spotlight. Blinking owlishly, the three of them

155

clambered into the Bus and took off.

"What the hell did you throw at them?"

"Magnesium flare," said Gideon. "There's nothing a Murk hates more than bright lights. Makes sense, since they're basically living shadows." He took a right out of the lot, tires chirping on the pavement. "You guys alright?"

"Yeah, I'm okay," said Tim. "They weren't trying to hurt us, just capture us." He hesitated. "Capture me, actually."

Gideon glanced back at Tim. "Why?"

"I have no idea." He sat back and looked at Vee, who was curled up in a ball against one wall of the van. "Hey, you okay?"

"Mmm-hmm." She was fiddling with the cuff of her sleeve and avoided looking at him. "Umm, you wanted to tell me something earlier, right?"

"Yeah."

"That was about the *vrolachi,* wasn't it?"

"Yeah, it was." A little knot of resentment formed in Tim's stomach.

"So," —she continued to fiddle— "the weaving I felt earlier, right after lunch. That wasn't you just practicing, was it?" She finally looked up at him. "You ran into one?"

"Yeah. Kyle was waiting for me in the bathroom."

Vee looked down again and chewed on her lip. "So, if I had listened to you instead of flying off the handle, we could've avoided all this?"

Tim realized she was working her way toward some sort of apology. "Well, I dunno. They were waiting for us."

"Yeah, but at least we would have been ready if I

hadn't been acting so stupid. If it weren't for the Guardian link I have with Gids. . ." She trailed off and looked up at Tim again. "I'm sorry."

The van fishtailed to a stop.

"OWWW!! Jesus, Gideon, where did you learn to drive?" Vee extricated herself from the corner she'd slid into, and Tim disentangled himself from some blankets. Gideon whipped open the curtains and stared down at his twin.

"Who are you and where the hell is my sister?"

"What?" Vee looked as confused as Tim felt.

"You apologized."

Vee rolled her eyes dramatically. "Oh, don't be an ass."

"You *never* apologize. For anything. Ever."

"That is so not true!"

"She shoved me off the end of a pier once," he said to Tim. "Broke two toes. Never apologized."

"We were seven! Oh my goddess, I can't believe—"

"She spoiled a surprise birthday present for our mom."

"That was *not* my fault, I thought you were ditching class."

"She ruined Santa for me."

"That was for your own good.

"So obviously," —he turned to Tim— "you must be a Mitternachten spy and she's under your mind control. Only possible explanation."

Vee chucked a pillow at his head.

"I'm sorry too," said Tim once he stopped laughing.

"Tim," said Vee, "you have nothing to apologize

for."

"Yes, I do." Tim stared down at his scarred hand, his right thumb running over the knuckles. "You're my friend. You're both my friends, and I trust you." He smiled faintly. "Kinda freakish how much I trust you. I've kept people out for so long, I'm still learning how to let people in. But you two deserve better from me. You've done so much for me in just the last few days." He looked up at Vee. "So, I will accept your apology if you accept mine."

She smiled and nodded. "I'm cool with that."

"So what now?" asked Gideon.

"Tim," Vee began, "do you have any idea, any at all why they were after you?"

"Nothing, unless it has something to do with my dad."

"Makes no sense," said Gideon. "What would a Midnighter want with a Denier?"

"How do you know a Midnighter's involved?"

"Murks are chaotic," explained Vee. "They never work together unless they're forced to. If that many are cooperating, there's got to be a Midnighter involved. A strong one."

"Yeah, Kyle mentioned something about orders."

"Exactly," said Vee.

"But, we can fight, right?"

"No." Gideon shook his head. "We can't."

"What?" Tim looked from one twin to the other. "But I've seen what you guys can do."

"And I've seen what Murks can do." Vee shook her head. "They were toying with us. If they'd wanted us dead, we'd be ribbons right now. They're deadly, and we're outnumbered four to one, if not more"

"We have to go to Kieran," said Gideon, "and bring Tim to Argent House again. He'll be safest there."

"We can't run."

"Why not?"

"Because I know what they're going to do next."

The twins stopped and stared at Tim.

"How do you know?" asked Vee.

"Because that thing inside Kyle pretty much told us, remember?"

Vee thought for a second, then her eyes widened. "You know if we go, we will be walking into a trap, right?"

"Yeah," Tim said softly, "I know."

"I'm lost," said Gideon. "What are they going to do?"

Tim swallowed and took a deep breath.

"They're going after my mother."

Chapter 17

"I hope this works," said Tim nervously. He pulled out his phone and started texting.

—*Hey, Mom, got a sec?*—
—*For you? Always. Detention done?* —
—*Yeah.* —
—*Last time, right?* —
—*Right. Listen, can you get off early?* —
—*I suppose. Why?* —

Tim took a deep breath before replying.

—*Remember I told you yesterday that jock and his friends were waiting for me?* —
—*OMG, did you get into another fight??? Are you OK???* —
—*Mostly. I think I messed up my wrist again. Might want to get it looked at. Sorry*—
—*Not your fault. RU at home?* —
—*On my way now.* —
—*Meet you there in 15 min. Love you.* —
—*Thanks. Sorry. Love you.* —

"God, I hate lying to her." Tim tucked his phone back into his pocket. They were idling in a parking space a few storefronts down from where Anna worked. As they waited, thick storm clouds started massing in the west, rolling ominously toward them. Vee craned her head over the back of the front seats to look up at the clouds.

"That could be good or bad."

"Why?"

"You've never had a chance to weave during a thunderstorm." She glanced back over her shoulder at Tim and smirked. "All of the elements are concentrated in them. You can tap into one and use it to juice up whatever you are doing. Storms supercharge everything. Of course," —she sat back with a sigh— "everything also means the Midnighter and their Murk buddies as well."

"*Vrolachi* can weave?"

"Only Darkness. You know, living shadows and all."

"Makes sense." Tim thought for a moment about what he'd sensed while the Murks had them. "How did they sever our weaves, then? I thought the only way to do that was by using the opposite element."

"Darkness is inherently destructive," said Gideon from the front seat. "That's its strength and its weakness; it doesn't play well with others."

"So it can't be woven in with other elements?"

"Nothing complicated, or only damaging stuff, from what I understand. It also means their weaves are easier to sever, if you're lucky enough to hit the right spot."

"What do you mean, lucky enough?"

"Well," said Vee, "you felt the shadow tentacles, right? Nothing but a big, cold blank, no way to know where to attack the weave. So you just have to guess and hope to knock something loose."

"A blank? That's not—"

"Is that her?" Gideon pointed out the window.

Tim leaned forward and saw his mom hustling out

of the office, juggling keys, purse, briefcase and coffee. She tossed everything but the coffee into the front seat, hurried around to the driver's side, got in, and almost got into an accident while pulling out. Tim's gut twisted with guilt.

"Okay, keep her in sight, but don't get too close."

"Yeah, because you have all the experience with tailing people, Mr. I'm Too Young To Drive." Gideon pulled out into traffic, and kept a few cars between them and Anna's car.

"So what's the plan?" Vee joined Tim in staring over the front seat.

"What do you mean?"

"The plan. The plan of what happens when we get to your house? Assuming we get that far."

"I have no idea. I hadn't thought that far ahead."

"Well we have to get our story straight," said Gideon. "If we get to your house, fine, we give her some story, but what if we run into the Murks? Even if we get away, what do we tell her?"

Tim was baffled. "I got nuthin'. Vengeful drug-addled jocks?"

"Maybe, but remember, we have to be careful about weaving around her. Nothing overt."

Tim's heart sank. "Do they have the same problem too? Are they hamstrung by the Unbelieving like we are?"

"I don't know!" Vee ran her fingers through her hair and sighed. When she spoke again it was much more gentle. "I don't know, Tim. I'm not some Amazon warrior chick with all the answers. I'm just…me."

"I know, it's just that," —he smiled and shook his head— "a small army of shadow-possessed football players want to kidnap my mother, and me and my punk-rock friends are going to fight them off with magic. This is completely nuts."

"Yeah." She reached out and put a hand on his shoulder. "I guess it is."

Then there was a squeal and a crunch, and Gideon swerved toward the curb, swearing fluently in Housetongue. Before the Bus was even stopped, Tim was grabbing the door handle. Outside was a mess. Another vehicle, a late-model SUV, had T-boned his mother's car as it went through an intersection. Already, teens in familiar letter jackets were climbing out, gathering around the wreck of Anna's car. Blind rage washed over Tim and he charged, forming the fighting weave Vee had shown him as he ran. The *vrolachi* sensed his weaving and turned, but not in time. Tim went airborne and kicked one in the chest hard enough to send him flying over the hood of the car, then pivoted and roundhoused another without touching the ground. A third got in one swing before Tim bounced him off the SUV with a blast of Air, then slammed him to the ground. He turned to see Vee and Gideon take down the other two. He hurried to the driver's side of the car.

"Mom? MOM!" Anna was unconscious, blood running down the left side of her face from a cut above her hairline; the window spiderwebbed from where her head had struck it. The door was crushed, so Tim placed his fingertips against the glass, wove Air, and pulled sharply outward. The safety glass shattered into tiny cubes and scattered across the pavement.

"Tim, move, let me see her." Vee pushed past him, already weaving some crazy complex thing he couldn't follow. She started passing her hands up and down above Anna's unconscious form.

"Sprained wrist," she muttered, "bad bruising on the left leg, laceration on her head, concussion, no fracture, neck is fine. We can move her." Gideon grabbed the doorframe, wove Earth and Fire into himself, wrenched the mangled door open, and gently lifted Anna out.

"How far is your house?" asked Vee.

"Just a few more blocks, we're almost there." Tim pointed.

"Let's get her in the van."

By the time they loaded Anna up, the sky had darkened significantly and the wind had picked up, flailing the branches around. Every hair on Tim's body stood at attention, and he could almost see the strands of the elements streaming by on the wind. How had he never noticed that before? He held his mother's hand as Gideon drove, and Vee sat with Anna's head in her lap, her head bowed and eyes closed, weaving the same complicated patterns Tim remembered from yesterday.

"Two blocks down, hang a right," he called to Gideon, "third block, left hand side on the corner. Big brown house, you can't miss it."

"She's gonna be okay," said Vee softly without looking up. "I can't do too much, especially for a Sleeper, but she's not that bad."

"My fault," Tim said.

"What are you talking about?" She looked up at last. "What would have happened if we hadn't been there?"

"My fault it happened. My fault you're involved, all of OWWWW!!" Tim's ear burned where Vee had snapped it with a weave of Air so quick, he didn't even see it.

"Shut. Up." She lowered her head again. "Gideon and I aren't here because you forced us to be. We're here because we are your friends and because this is our job. Protect people. Find potentials. Fight back against the Darkness. That's what we do, that's what we trained to do since we were kids. As for your mom, I'm sure she'd take a few bumps on the head to protect her family. So it's not all about you, you know."

"If you want to blame someone," said Gideon from the front, "put it on the one who deserves it."

"The Midnighter," said Tim grimly.

"Bingo."

"Holy crap," muttered Gideon. "Dude, is that your house?"

Tim sighed and smiled. He'd been expecting this. "Yeah, hang on, let me open the gate." He pulled out his phone, opened an app, and put his thumb to the screen. Vee gave him a look.

"What do you mean, open the gate?"

"Just go look, it's easier."

Vee eased out from under Anna's head and leaned over the front seat. She looked up, swore softly in Housetongue, then leaned back and fixed Tim with an incredulous smile.

"You live in a castle?"

The Hansen house was a Victorian enormity of peaked roofs, arches, and towers on a double lot, all done in brown fieldstone, towering a full story over the not-inconsiderable houses nearby. A tall wrought-iron fence surrounded the property, and massive oaks arched over the well-kept grounds, full of shady nooks and greenery. As the Bus slipped through the gate, Tim thumbed the app again and it closed behind them with a hum and a clang. At the sound, Vee jumped as though she'd been goosed, and Tim rubbed his arms unconsciously.

"Did you feel that?" asked Vee.

"Feel what?"

"Proof that your dad really is a Denier. There are old weaves in the fence, defensive stuff. Didn't you feel them activate when the gate closed?"

"Yeah, I guess I did." He'd always felt that chill when the gates closed, even as a kid. Now he knew why.

"Well congrats," chimed in Gideon, "your castle is protected by magic spells."

"C'mon," said Vee, "let's get your mom inside before the guests arrive."

Chapter 18

Perhaps it was the storm, or the gloom, or the stress of the day, but Tim got an unpleasant sense of déjà vu the moment he set foot into the empty house. He half expected to hear a tree branch crash through the front window. As Gideon eased Anna down onto the couch, Tim flipped the light switch. Nothing. The sense of flashback redoubled. Vee knelt to check on her patient.

"She's probably going to be out for a while, but her leg and concussion are mending nicely." She straightened and released her weave. "She'll wake up sore but not much more than that."

"You're amazing." To Tim's surprise, Vee blushed a bit.

"Hey, guys," Gideon called from the front room, "you better come here."

They hurried to join him at the front window. Gathered around the gate were at least two dozen figures. Most were tall and athletic, but the one in the center was broad and heavy, wearing a long overcoat and carrying some sort of cane or staff. Looking at him made something in Tim's memory buzz.

"There's so many of them," said Vee in a small voice. "There's no way we can fight that many at once."

"We may not have to," said Gideon, and he walked away from the window and into the dining room.

"We're going to do something way crazier." Outside, the storm rumbled.

Vee stopped and stared at her brother. "That might work," she said after a second. "It also might blow up in our faces, but it might work."

"What's the plan?" Tim asked.

"The storm," Gideon explained. "If we can tap into it, we can use it to reinforce the defensive weaves on the fence. The problem is, mucking about in someone else's weaving is risky. Plus, the weaves are old, and they will be tapping into the storm too. If they do break through—"

"Feedback loop," Vee finished. "It would blow the defensive weaves to hell, and probably worse."

"Worse how, exactly?"

"It would feed back into us, like an electrical circuit. Literally, since we are talking about a thunderstorm." Vee's face was pale, but set.

"Do we have any other choice?" asked Tim.

Vee shook her head slowly. "Not really."

Tim nodded. "Show me what to do."

Vee held out her hands to both boys. They joined hands in a circle just as the first peal of thunder rattled the windows. A wave of goosebumps shot down Tim's spine, too much to be attributed to the storm.

"He's already tapping in, we need to hurry. It's just like healing; open yourself to the elements and I will draw through you both." Tim closed his eyes, reached out to the storm overhead, and breathed the power in. Instantly, a torrent of elemental energy poured into him, so much he half-expected to start floating off the floor.

"Maiden, Mother, and Crone," muttered Gideon, "Tim, what the hell, dude!"

"Told ya," Vee said softly, "now shut up." Tim felt her draw though both of them and extend outward. Through her, he felt the entire house come alive, like an extension of their bodies. The fence felt like a netting of light, an incredibly complex tapestry of interwoven strands, but here and there some of the threads were faded, grayed out, even black and dead. More surprising, there were dozens of other old weaves throughout the house, all seeming to center in the very room they occupied.

"Tim, there's decades of old weavings here. How is that…" Another crack of thunder interrupted Vee's question, and a black force threw itself at the barrier, worming its way into the weakened areas.

"Oh no you don't, you bastard!" muttered Vee through her teeth. She drew harder through the boys and started threading filaments into the barrier, reinforcing the darkening areas with bright new energy. Immediately, Tim felt the Midnighter counterattack, shifting to undefended patches, but Vee kept pace with every move, weaving and tying off faster than Tim could follow. She couldn't repair any more areas, but she seemed to be keeping his damage at bay.

"It's working," Gideon growled.

"Yeah." Vee panted. "But he's so quick."

"I have an idea," said Tim. Just like before, Vee wasn't drawing on his full capacity. He split his focus, holding his connection to the circle while probing into the myriad other old weaves in the house. He quickly found what he was hoping for; an old structure of Earth and Fire, twining directly toward the gate. He formed his own weave, mirroring the original pattern, and fitted the two together. They interlaced like lock and key, and the weave flared to life. A ripple of power surged toward the gate, and outside there was a scarlet flash and a *WHUMP* that made the chandelier above them tremble. The assault on the shield suddenly vanished.

"What did you just do?" asked Gideon.

"Best defense is a good offense." Tim smiled. "I figured there had to be more than just barriers protecting this house, there had to be some offensive weaves as well. Looks like I was right."

"Nice! Hopefully that will buy us a breather."

"I'm working as fast as I can," Vee said, "but I don't think that bought us much time."

As if on cue, the attack renewed itself, but now from a dozen directions at once.

"The *vrolachi,* they must have surrounded the house." Vee stopped drawing through Tim and Gideon. "We need to split our focus, cover as much area as we can. Keep the circle connected so we can help each other out."

Quick as they could, the three counterattacked, lashing out at the tendrils of Darkness that wormed away at the thin points of the shield. But with each retaliation, the Murks retreated, then moved to another weak point, and another, and another.

"What are they doing?" hissed Vee in frustration.

"I don't know," said Gideon. "It doesn't make any sense! It's like they're not really trying, like—"

"They're just distracting us," Tim finished. He shifted his focus back to the gate and sensed exactly what he'd feared—a weave extending from the gate directly into the heart of the storm.

"NO!" Desperately, Tim lashed out, trying to sever the Midnighter's structure, but he was a second too late.

A flash lit up the world, thunder seemed to split the air apart, and the defensive shield shattered like crystal. A massive backlash of energy traveled along Tim's severing weave and through the circle to Gideon and Vee, knocking all three teens senseless.

And the storm finally broke.

****

Daniel Lum stood, staff grounded in front of him, examining his handiwork, perfectly dry and comfortable inside a weave of Air and Water. Before him, the gate stood open, smoking and twisted, still glowing where the lightning bolt had struck. That had been astonishingly close; he never ceased to be surprised at Tim's abilities. A second earlier, and he could have easily disrupted Dan's weave, which could have been disastrous in many different ways. Luckily, the gate and shield had taken the full brunt of the assault, with just enough backlash to put the three of them exactly where the Midnighter wanted them, incapacitated but not truly harmed. He smiled at his good fortune.

"You four," —he gestured vaguely at the now-sopping-wet group of jocks behind him— "drop the meatsuits and head inside. It should be more than dark enough in there for you to shadowstep now."

"Yes, Master," said the Kyle-thing. "I know Freakshow is off-limits, but may we play with the other two?" The hunger in his voice was obvious.

"Not yet. Meneleas' twins are not vital to my plan, but may be useful as leverage. But I need you to handle this a certain way. Listen…"

****

Tim sat up, his head still swimming from the

backlash. Gideon and Vee still lay on the dining room floor, unmoving. Rain lashed the windows, so he could not have been out for very long. If anything, it was darker now than when they'd arrived.

Dark. Shadows. *Vrolachi.*

"Guys." Tim scuttled over and shook Vee's shoulder. "You gotta wake up, you gotta wake up *right now.*"

"Freeeeeekshow."

The voice was not even vaguely human. It sounded like fallen leaves skittering across dead grass formed into words.

"You're all alone, Freakshow. No Dusker twins to help you, nowhere to run to, and little Mommy all tuckered out with a bump on her head."

"Don't you touch them!"

Click. Click. Click.

Something was walking slowly down the hall. Something with claws.

In a panic, Tim wove Air and Fire and tossed a sphere of light toward the sound. It hit the wall and exploded like soundless fireworks, dazzling him.

Silence. Then a skittering sound, which Tim thought might be laughter. Outside another peal of thunder sounded.

"The brightest lights make the darkest shadows, whelp." From the left.

"More places for us to hide." Ahead, in the stairwell.

"More places to pop out of." Directly behind him, almost in his ear. Tim whirled but saw nothing. Again, the skittering laughter.

"Come out and face me!" Tim meant for it to

sound strong and defiant but even to his own ears he sounded terrified. A white-blue flash of lightning sliced through the windows, thickening the shadows.

"Is that what you really want, Freakshow? To look a vrolach *in the face?"* From the doorway straight ahead. Click. Click. Click.

"Oh god," whispered Tim, and it came into view.

It was vaguely humanoid, but the proportions were so off it hurt Tim's brain to look at it. Dead black, so black it seemed more like a void than a thing with mass, arms stick-thin and so long they nearly dragged on the ground, attached to the massive, hunched shoulders of a gorilla. But the worst was its head, jutting forward on a long, almost snake-like neck, the face featureless but for a single, flat white eye, without pupil or iris. It skitter-laughed again.

"What, no words for my beauty? No matter, you'll soon be squealing instead, you and your little Dusker friendsssss." As it hissed out the last word, three more *vrolachi* stepped out of the shadows surrounding Tim, each more horrifically misshapen than the last.

I am going to die, thought Tim, and they rushed him.

Tim squeezed his eyes shut and hurled another firework at his feet, hoping to blind them. He tried to bolt toward the living room, but freezing blades slashed across his back and he stumbled and fell. He rolled just in time to catch one with a weave of Air as it leaped at him, but instead of crashing into the ceiling the Murk simply evaporated into the shadows. He scrambled up but a blow caught him in the ribs, driving the wind from his lungs and sending him sliding across the floor and into an end table. His head rang, but he felt them

173

weaving Darkness, summoning the shadow tentacles to bind him again. Tim counterattacked, severing weaves with everything he had, and for a heartbeat he held his own. Then another blindside blow caught him behind the knees, and in that moment of distraction he was bound again. He continued to fight, but for every tendril of blackness he cut, three more took their place. Soon he was trussed like a fly in a web. The first *vrolach,* the one he thought had been inside Kyle Peterson, gestured, and the tentacles lifted Tim up until he was face to face with the Murk.

"What are you, Freakshow?" Its mocking cruelty had vanished, replaced by a quiet, cold menace. *"You sever our shadow, no Dusker can do this."* It gripped Tim's face in one frigid, long-fingered hand, its claws digging into his cheeks. Tim reached desperately for the elements, but every attempt was blocked by the other *vrolachi.* He stretched out with his mind, harder, deeper, and felt…something.

"Tell me what you are, whelp, and I will give you to my master quickly. Refuse," —it seemed to smile at him— *"and we play first."*

"Go." Tim reached for this new thing, which seemed to be beneath the other elements.

"To." He drew it into himself, and was filled with a cold fire. The *vrolach* cocked its head, as though it heard a strange noise.

"HELL!" With every bit of his strength, Tim twisted this new power into a piercing blade and drove it directly into the *vrolach's* blank, white eye. It shrieked in agony, a high, whispery screech that dug into Tim's ears like a drill bit, stumbled back three steps, and exploded into a cloud of black motes. For a

heartbeat, all of them stared at the spot where the Kyle-thing had stood, then the three remaining *vrolachi* turned slowly back toward Tim, hissing, their flat eyes full of fury.

Now *I'm going to die*, thought Tim. Every tendril around his body suddenly tightened, crushing the air from his lungs. One slipped around his throat and squeezed, making him gag out his last wisp of air. He panicked, struggling, spots dancing in front of his vision, and something in Tim's rib cage gave way with an agonizing pop. His pulse pounded in his head.

And a small, slight figure rose up behind the *vrolachi.*

Vee, though Tim dimly. *About time you woke up.*

A weapon appeared in her hand, long and spear-like, shining a soft blue-white, and she attacked, cutting down the first Murk before they even realized she was there. Some of the tendrils released, but the one around Tim's throat tightened even more, and blackness started to close in around the edges of his vision. He could barely see her now, a slim silhouette, moving like a dancer, fighting both Murks at once. She ducked under an attack and gestured, and one of the *vrolachi* burst into flame, flew upward, and crashed into the ceiling before dissolving into black motes. The last tried to meld into the shadows, but she threw her spear with such force that the Murk was lifted off its feet and impaled on the wall like a bug on a pin. The last of the shadow tentacles evaporated, and Tim collapsed to the floor, gagging and heaving great, agonizing, glorious breaths.

"Tim." Footsteps approached him, and cool hands cupped his face. "Timmy, honey, sit up, let me help you." He raised his head, and his heart nearly stopped in shock. For it was not Vee Melan who had saved him, who had killed three *vrolachi* in a matter of seconds.

It was Anna Hansen, his mother.

Chapter 19

"Mom?" It came out as a whispery croak.

"Shh, don't talk, kiddo." She ran her hands up and down over his body, scanning him for injuries just as Vee had done for her after the accident. Tim's skin buzzed and tingled in response. He stared at her, dumbfounded.

"We need to get you fixed up. Has anyone healed you before? Do you know how to help?" Tim tried to speak, winced in pain, and nodded. He reached out for the elements, and she gasped in surprise.

"So strong." She sounded both proud and sad. She placed her hands gingerly on either side of his neck, drew in through him, and started weaving with such speed and delicacy that it made Vee look slow and fumble-fingered. The healing warmth spread from his neck through his whole body, and he took a deep, grateful breath.

"Better?" She brushed a strand of hair out of his eyes and kissed him on the forehead.

"Mom, what—"

"Not now, kiddo." She stood up, brushed off her hands, and looked up and behind Tim, a grim smile on her face. "I need to ask someone some questions."

She walked around Tim, and as he turned he realized who, or what, she meant; the Murk she'd impaled was still alive. It struggled feebly, grasping at the shaft of his mother's weapon with its too-long fingers, inky blood dripping onto the carpet. But it was the weapon itself that truly caught Tim's attention. Whatever it was made from, it had no name in this world. Perhaps four feet long, a third of that a broad, double-edged blade, it was all of one piece, crystalline blue striated with white and still glowing faintly. It looked like nothing so much as a piece of a summer sky forged into a weapon. As he stared, he had the not-quite-comfortable feeling he was looking *into* it rather than at it.

Anna approached the pinned *vrolach*, seemingly unafraid. She tilted her head to one side, as though admiring the scene, and wrapped one hand around the haft of the spear.

"*One chance, night-maggot,*" she said in Housetongue. Her grip tightened, and the entire weapon shifted from blue-white to red-tinged gray, and the Murk stiffened in pain, its feet tattooing against the wall. Her hand relaxed, and the spear regained its normal appearance.

"Who?" Anna said simply.

"*...you...know...who, Corruptor,*" it gasped out. "*He...will be...pleased.*" It hissed out what Tim thought might be a weak laugh. Anna's face twisted with fury. She gripped the spear again, this time weaving Air and Fire. Electricity arced up and down the weapon, the Murk gave one brief scream before dissolving into motes of blackness.

"Damn him," said Anna softly. "Damn him to the blackest of hells and back." She pulled her spear from the wall with a crunch, and then glanced at Tim.

"Stand back, kiddo." She set the haft of the spear

on the floor between her feet, and started drawing elemental energies the likes of which Tim had never even imagined. Now, at last, he had an idea of how the twins felt around him. He could not have held even a fraction of what she now wielded, and yet there was no effort on her face. She wove all of it into a sphere of incredible complexity, raised her spear butt off the floor, and drove it down. The sphere exploded outward, passing around and through Tim like an electric wind, embedding itself into the walls of the house. He now understood what she had done. She had recreated the same defensive shield that the Midnighter had shattered, just on a smaller scale. The very one whose complexity had stymied he and the twins, and she'd remade it in less than 30 seconds.

"Oh…my…goddess."

Tim turned and saw Vee and Gideon standing in the doorway, both wearing expressions that bordered on religious awe.

"That…" Gideon pointed at Anna's spear. "That's an aiglos." He swallowed and blinked. "That's an aiglos, your mother has an aiglos, that's not possible, she—"

He never finished the sentence. A weave of Air from Anna picked them both up, dragged them across the room, slammed them into the wall the Murk had so recently occupied and pinned them there.

"Mom, what are you doing? These are my friends!" Anna wove again and an invisible wall slammed into place between them. Tim tried to sever it, but the weave was so intricate he couldn't find where to begin. He slammed a fist against it in frustration. "Stop!"

Anna advanced slowly toward the bound twins.

179

Gideon simply stared in shock, but Vee tried to speak.

"My lady, please, we didn't…"

"You stupid," Anna cut in. "Half-trained. Children. Do you have any idea what you've done? How much damage you've caused?" She raised her aiglos with one hand and held the tip level with Vee's throat. "Or perhaps that was deliberate?"

Gideon continued to stare, but Vee's expression hardened. "I am the daughter of the First Speaker of Avalon. Even you should be careful what you accuse me of."

Anna immediately lowered her weapon, her anger replaced with shock. The weaves holding all three teens dissolved.

"Mel," Anna whispered. She looked at the twins with a slight smile on her face. "You're Mel's twins. The last time I saw you…"

The doorbell rang.

The sound, after all the abnormality, froze all four of them. The teens all turned to look at Anna simultaneously. She took a deep breath, let it out, smoothed down the front of her suit coat, brushed a strand of hair away from her face, and turned toward the front door. As she approached it, she held out her aiglos and released it, but instead of falling to the floor, it dissolved into a shimmer of blue sparks and disappeared.

"Mom, I don't think you want to open that door." She paused with her hand on the doorknob and looked back at him over one shoulder.

"I know that I don't," she said simply, and turned the knob.

On the doorstep stood Dan Lum, smiling

pleasantly, hands clasped behind him, his eyes black-scarlet and twenty *vrolachi*-possessed football players on the lawn behind him.

"Annika," he said, "it's been a long time."

"Naldumiel." Anna crossed her arms. "Not long enough."

"Dan?!" cried Vee in shock.

"Dr. Lum?!" Tim echoed. Gideon said nothing, only stood there.

Anna turned and looked at them, puzzled, then closed her eyes with a pained expression.

"Daniel Lum," she said slowly, "an anagram. Really? Could you get any more cliché?"

"It's a classic." Naldumiel shrugged. "And I enjoyed leaving you little hints, even though I knew you couldn't get them. Call me a narcissist."

"You *are* a narcissist. *And* a sociopath. And a *murderer*, for that matter."

"From your perspective," the Midnighter replied as though the subject bored him.

"What do you want?"

"Eventually?" He gestured with his chin toward the twins. "Your head on a spike right next to their father's, Avalon in flames, and your brilliant son back where he belongs. But for now?" He grinned without humor. "I just want to gloat."

"Mom? What's going on? How do you know Dan?"

"Because your parents made a deal with me."

"Don't you *dare* speak to him!!"

"Or what?" He flicked a finger against the barrier, which shimmered slightly and gave off a crystal bell sound. "This keeps me out, but it also keeps you in.

You break the barrier, " —he gestured behind him to his minions— "you're amazing, Annika, but even you can't hold off twenty *vrolachi* and keep three other people safe at the same time." He glanced upward and around the doorframe. "This barrier really is brilliant work, my dear, you've lost none of your—"

"Shut up."

The Midnighter smiled at Tim. He held up one hand, and swirls of what looked like smoke started twining around his fingers. Tim felt another of those nails-on-chalkboard chills, and he shuddered involuntarily. Naldumiel's smile widened.

"You can feel it when I do this, can't you?"

Tim crossed his arms. "So what if I can?"

"They can't." He gestured toward Tim's companions. Sure enough, the twins were staring at him in shock, while Anna couldn't meet his eyes. "Can you figure out why? C'mon, Tim, use that big brain of yours."

Tim thought of everything his Dusker friends had told him, everything he'd felt around the Murks, and of the strange attack he'd used to destroy the one *vrolach,* and the truth dawned on him. He looked at his feet, the implications of it all crashing like a wave through his mind.

"My dad…he is a Denier. But he wasn't a Dusker, was he?" He looked up at Naldumiel. "He was Mitternachten."

"NO!" Anna (or, Tim wondered, is it Annika now?) grabbed Tim's shoulders and turned him to face her. "Do not listen to him! He just wants to—"

"Is it true?"

"Tim."

"Is it true?"

Annika bowed her head, and nodded. "Yes."

"But you're a Denier too. How are you okay, while Dad isn't?"

"Because your parents aren't typical," said Naldumiel. Annika gave him a glare that could have cracked stone. "By all means, my dear, tell him yourself if you think my version would be biased."

"The Ban of the Lethe," she said softly. "It's a ritual. Your father and I..." She hesitated and walked away from the door for a moment. "We wouldn't have been simply outcasts. We would have been hunted, by both sides, because of who we were."

"Which is what, exactly?"

"Heroes," said Gideon. Everyone turned to him, surprised.

"I was going to say champions," said Annika. "It doesn't feel very heroic from the inside. We were leaders of each side, rivals, the faces of this chapter of the endless war between Dusk and Midnight. For us to then fall in love with each other? To say we couldn't just walk away is a massive understatement."

"So they came to me," said the Midnighter.

"I thought this was my story to tell," snapped Annika.

"You suck at it," he snapped back. "The Ban of the Lethe is a ritual that completely removes someone, or in this case, two someones, from otherworldly knowledge and existence. Memory, ability to weave, history— everything is changed, and not just in the subjects of the ritual. They become myths and legends in the minds of those who knew them, and their entire memories are rewritten. And since it is a specialty of the

Mitternachten and you cannot cast it on yourself, they needed my help."

"The deal you mentioned."

"Exactly."

"But why you?" To Tim's surprise, the expression on Naldumiel's face softened, and his eyes faded over to their original sea-green color.

"Because your father is my oldest friend. We grew up together." He looked at Annika. "Now, would you like to finally tell your son why his father is slowly losing his mind?"

"The Ban," said Annika, "is a creation of the Midnighters because they need it. Darkness isn't like the other elements. It corrupts you."

"I prefer to think of it as transforming, but please, continue."

"Walking away from this life, from the weaving of the elements, is hard enough for a Dusker, but for a Midnighter it is literally impossible. Weaving Darkness changes you physiologically. So the only way to do it is to lock it away from the user completely. And even then," —she hesitated again— "it's not foolproof."

"I warned you." Naldumiel's voice was thick with bitterness. "Sixteen years ago I warned you. I told you what the chances were of it working. I told you what the consequences would be if, no, *when* the Ban began to fail. For all that time, the Longing has been eating away at Vittorio's mind. Look at the result!" He gestured toward Tim. "Even if you care nothing for the well-being of the man you supposedly love, look at your son's face! At his hand! That is the result of the two of you flaunting the laws of both our societies! Well..." He straightened and adjusted his overcoat. "I decided to take matters into my own hands."

"So you decided to attack me?" Tim was surprised at how sharply that came out.

"The Ban is hellishly difficult to break, Tim. Even putting the person in danger isn't enough. There is only one sure way to destroy it, and that's to put a loved one of a Banned person in a life-threatening position. The instinct to help or protect them is the only thing powerful enough to shatter the ritual."

"So you decided to attack me?"

"Ask your friends, Tim. If either of them had been trapped in a house with four Murks, they'd be dead in seconds."

"So you decided—"

"Don't bother, Tim." Annika came up and put a hand on his shoulder. "He's very good at pretending to be a normal person, but in truth, he cares about nothing and no one but himself."

"And what about you, Annika no Titania Serafi?" snarled the Midnighter. "The mighty warrior, the great general, wielder of one of the seven aigloi, now so reviled by your own people that they will not even speak your name! Every bridge you had is burnt, every friend has forgotten you. You have no place in any world, and why? Because you and Vittorio thought that the rules wouldn't apply to you." He blew air out through his nose and seemed to compose himself. He turned to Tim. "But that is not the case for you."

"What do you mean?"

"Avalon will not embrace you, Tim. You will be as hated as your mother, and for reasons that are completely not your fault. Do you want to live like that? Would anyone?" He stepped closer. "You are as much a Child of Midnight as you are of Dusk. I am an influential man. There could be a place for you amongst my people, if you want it." Tim was surprised at the earnestness in the older man's voice. He shrugged his mom's hand off his shoulder and walked directly up to the door.

"Let me get this straight," he said, businesslike. "You want me to ditch my mom, the woman who raised me and took care of me and loved me. You want me to drop the first real friends I've ever had and not only never speak to them again, but become their enemy. You want me to go off to someplace that I've never been, with you, a guy who I've had one real conversation with, the guy who just admitted to me that he had demons attack me just to break a magic spell. And you want me to do this just so I can avoid being an outsider, something I've already been for my entire life?" Tim leaned forward until he was inches from the barrier. "In what *universe* did you think I would actually say yes?"

A blast of black fire erupted against the doorway, and Tim stumbled backward. The fire died as quickly as it came, revealing a furious Naldumiel.

"Do you think this is a game, boy? Do you think this is a school, where you can coast by on attitude? This is war, and the Opacaroi will lose! I offer you a chance to survive, and you throw it back in my face? So be it, you are obviously your mother's son."

"What are you implying?" asked Annika. "What about the war?"

"Let's just say," the Midnighter said, his smug attitude reasserting itself, "that things have progressed while you've been gone." A musical tone sounded from

Naldumiel's pocket. He pulled out his phone, thumbed at it for a moment, and smiled. "Well," he said as he slipped it back into his pocket, "this has been fascinating, but I have more pressing matters to attend to." He turned to leave.

"Where are you going, Naldumiel?" For the first time there was a hint of fear in Annika's voice.

"Oh, I think you know. Did you think I was hanging out on your porch for the scintillating conversation?" He turned his collar up against the tapering drizzle. "But I will leave some friends with you to keep you company. Wouldn't want you to get lonely, would I?" He turned to one of the possessed jocks. "If they come out that door, kill them all." He glanced back. "The little ones first." He turned back and set the butt of his staff on the ground. "Annika, if I ever see you again, I will happily kill you. Tim," —he hesitated, and something like real regret crossed his face— "you're a fool." He turned, stepped into the shadows of the nearby trees, and disappeared.

Chapter 20

The instant Naldumiel left, Annika slammed the door and threw the bolt with a hard, final thunk. She leaned against it and smiled grimly.

"I cannot wait to kill that man," she muttered, then stalked past the teens and toward the stairs.

"Mom, what are we going to do?"

"*We* aren't going to do anything," she said without turning. "*I* am going to go save your father and you and your little friends are going to go someplace safe." She started up the stairs.

"What do you mean, save Dad?"

"Naldumiel is going to Forestview."

"What? Why?" Tim followed her up.

"If I had to guess, to kidnap your father." She rounded the landing.

"Then I'm coming with you."

Annika stopped and turned. "Honey, there's no time to argue. Those *vrolachi* you fought? They were playing with you up until the end. You go with me, they won't hesitate to tear you apart, and I can't save your dad and protect you at the same time. I need you to stay safe."

"Would you?" She looked genuinely surprised at Tim's question. "Would you stay behind if Dad had to save me? Would Dad stay behind if I had to save you?"

"It's not the same, kiddo."

"It is for me." He walked up to the landing. "I can feel when they weave Darkness, remember? You can't. I can help you."

Annika stared at Tim for a heartbeat, then lowered her head and sighed.

"Timoteo ko Vittorio Serafi," she said softly, "do not make me regret this." It took Tim a moment to realize that she had just called him by his full Dusker name. She glanced down at where Vee and Gideon stood, almost forgotten in all the drama. "Can we trust them?" she asked softly.

"They saved my life. Twice."

Annika nodded. "Hey you two." They both jumped. "Can you fight at least a little?"

"I was top of my class at the House of Winds," said Vee, her voice a little too high, "and Gideon here has had full Guardian training." She hesitated before adding, "Ma'am."

Annika rolled her eyes slightly. "That'll have to do. I can't leave you behind when the Gray Council's thugs show up, and four is better than two, I suppose." She started back up the stairs. "We leave in three minutes!" She turned a corner, and Tim heard her bedroom door close.

"I need to sit down," said Vee breathlessly, and Gideon collapsed onto the bottom stair.

"What's with you two?"

Gideon opened his mouth, hesitated, and closed it. "How the hell do we explain this?"

"Your mom," Vee began, "she's like…a rock star and Public Enemy #1 rolled together. There's this old movie, Natural Born Killers. Have you ever seen it?"

"No," said Tim. "How have you seen it?"

"Pirated Wi-Fi and way too much time on our hands," Gideon mumbled.

"Anyway," Vee continued, "it's about these serial killers that become national celebrities. Really weird movie. But that's kinda what your mom is like to us. We grew up hearing about her, but they never used her name, I guess because of that Ban ritual thing. They call her the Betrayer, the Forgotten One, all this bad stuff, but there's also people who admire her. And…" She trailed off and looked embarrassed.

"What?"

But at that moment Annika came back down the stairs, and the twins immediately sprang to attention. This wasn't surprising because she was wearing something that looked like a military uniform: her hair braided and tucked under a brimmed cap, form-fitting pants with a multitude of pockets tucked into boots, a vest with more pockets over a knit long-sleeved shirt, all in shades of dark gray. Tim wasn't sure which was weirder, the outfit or the fact that she looked so at-home in it.

"Alright," she said, "let me set up a distraction and then we can go." She walked into the dining room and gestured broadly, weaving a multitude of different things at once. The carpet and all of the furniture swept aside and arranged itself against the wall, revealing a familiar design etched onto the floor; the sigil of the Opacaroi, perhaps eight feet across. Annika held her hand out above it and immediately the various sections began to glow. Her brow furrowed, and she cocked her head to one side.

"Who's been mucking about with the defenses?"

"Me," said Tim, "when we were trying to keep the

shield up."

"Good choice." She smiled. "But there were some better ones." She cocked her fingers into an odd position, then turned her hand like she was turning a key in a lock. Immediately, a slew of weaves flared to life around the house, and outside were a series of thuds, crackles, and raised voices. Annika's smile widened. "That should keep those Murks occupied until we can get on our way. C'mon." To Tim's surprise, she led them, not toward the garage, but to the kitchen.

"Where are we going?"

"Basement," she said simply. "Now you three listen up. Naldumiel thinks we are trapped here, or at least that it will take time for us to get past the Murks. If we can get to Forestview quickly enough, we can use that to our advantage." She opened the basement door and started down. "Once we get there, we need to do everything as quickly and quietly as possible. The sun should be down by the time we arrive, which means most likely the *vrolachi* won't be using hosts. It makes them more dangerous, but makes things much easier for us." She paused at the bottom, turned to face them, and wove a blade of Spirit and Fire, with a hint of the other elements. "Memorize this weave—it's the best thing to use against the Murks. A single strike with this to either the brain or heart should kill them instantly, but if you miss, the pain will probably drive it into a frenzy. So quick, quiet, and precise is absolutely necessary. Do you understand?"

"Yes, Ma'am," said Vee and Gideon in unison, and Tim nodded.

Annika turned and continued through the main room of the basement, opening a door on the back wall

Tim had never noticed before, though he thought he'd explored every nook and cranny of this house. As he stepped through it, he could sense weaves of distraction and illusion on the doorframe. It opened onto a dusty storeroom, walled in old fieldstone rather than concrete, full of crates and boxes and other brick-a-brack that Tim was sure predated their living there. To his surprise, an aetherlight, thick with cobwebs, sprung to life on the ceiling, bathing them in a gray-gold glow. His mom picked her way carefully to the back of the storeroom and placed her hand on a seemingly-random rock jutting from the wall. A thick grating sound filled the room, and a section of the wall swung inward, revealing a twisting staircase headed down, lined with more dusty aetherlights flickering in response to their presence. As Annika started down, Gideon turned to Tim.

"Dude," he whispered, "now it's official; coolest house *ever*."

"Shut up." Tim rolled his eyes, but smiled.

The staircase went down perhaps thirty steps, curving back on itself, then opened onto a chamber that looked to run the entire length of the house. It appeared to be a natural cave, though the ceiling had been buttressed here and there with stout wooden pillars. The moment Tim set foot into it, he was almost overwhelmed by the sense of power in the room. This place had seen weaving the likes of which he could barely contemplate.

In the center of the room a massive, slightly asymmetrical crystal of smoky quartz jutted from the floor, perhaps four feet tall and as thick around as a tree trunk. Every facet and surface of the crystal was etched with fine, spidery symbols, and looking at them gave Tim a strange, reverberating sensation in his mind, like when he'd first heard the twins speaking Housetongue. Vee took one look at the crystal and stopped dead in her tracks.

"You built your house on a leypoint?"

"Young lady," said Annika archly, "how old do you think I am?"

Vee stammered, blushed, and went silent, but Tim's mom just laughed softly.

"This cave has been a Dusker sanctuary for as far back as we have records. When the town started expanding about a hundred and fifty years ago, my great-grandfather built the house on top of the cave to protect it." She turned to Tim. "Leylines are conduits of elemental energy that crisscross the world. Places where they meet are called leypoints, and they are places of great power. Duskers use these crystals to focus the energy. And they have some other uses as well." She held her hand out over it but, Tim noticed, did not touch.

"I've heard about leyline traveling," said Gideon, "and I've heard it's not fun."

"That's putting it delicately." Annika eyed the crystal the way one looks at a necessary but highly unpleasant job, like unclogging a sink. "Alright, listen. There's a grove at one end of the Forestview grounds that we can travel to, but chances are Naldumiel used the same place as his staging area. I expect to drop directly into a fight with whatever rear guard they left behind, so remember what I told you. If we run into something human, subdue it. If it's not human, kill it, quick and quiet, no hesitation."

"What about whoever is helping the Midnighter?" asked Vee. "Whoever texted him?"

"You noticed that, huh?" Annika nodded in approval. "That means there's going to be at least one more Nightweaver there, plus the Crone only knows what kind of helpers. You have to be ready and you *cannot hesitate.*" She looked around at the teenagers. "Ready?"

They all nodded.

"Then circle up." All four clasped hands in a chain. As they opened themselves to the elements, Tim could sense the unique feel of each of their abilities: Gideon's slow strength, Vee's whip-quick accuracy, and his mother like a fractal storm.

"As much as I don't like this, Tim, you've got point. Keep your senses open and warn us the moment you feel anyone weaving anything, especially Darkness." She drew through all of them and began to weave, intertwining all of their energies and locking their hands together.. "Ready?"

"Yes, Ma'am," said Gideon.

"Yes, Ma'am," said Vee

Tim nodded. "Let's go get Dad."

"Hold on to your stomachs." She completed the weave and slapped her free hand down onto the crystal. Tim was immediately yanked off his feet so hard he thought both arms were going to dislocate, and iron bands seemed to squeeze down on him from every direction. The world became a kaleidoscopic blur of color; energies pummeled him from every side. They whipsawed every which way: left, right, right, up, down twice, faster and faster, each turn clamping down tighter and tighter.

And then they were through.

They landed in a jumbled heap on soft, wet grass, dark except for a faint reddish glow. Gideon rolled up onto his knees and was promptly sick.

"Every time," muttered Vee, and she started to get to her feet.

"GET DOWN!" Tim snagged her around the waist with a weave of Air and yanked her off her feet. A blast of red-black flame blasted directly through the space she'd occupied a split second earlier.

No hesitation.

Tim jumped up, weaving as he moved, first the combat senses, then forming the severing blades his mother had shown him. Three Murks stood just feet away, shellshocked, and something else was there too, something that was the source of the reddish glow, something that towered over them and looked like a walking forest fire. A raw wave of panic washed over him.

"*Utari!*" yelled Gideon.

The burning figure bellowed, a sound like a flamethrower in a well, and charged them. Tim ducked under a swinging arm and came up face to face with a shocked *vrolach*. He drove one of his weave-blades upward under its chin, and it exploded into motes. A second one started to fade into the shadows.

"Oh no you don't." He instinctively wove Darkness again, forming tendrils that whipped out and pulled the Murk back to him, where he pinned it to the ground with a blade. It squealed once and then vaporized. He turned in time to see Vee and Gideon double-team to take down the third Murk, and his mother...

Wow.

She was hovering ten feet off the ground, the *utari* trapped below her in a cyclone of Earth and Water. She summoned her aiglos and came hurtling down, splitting her opponent in two like firewood on a chopping block. Her weave disappeared and the *utari* stood for a moment, hissing and steaming, before collapsing into a pile of wet ash. Annika stood from her crouch position, rolled her neck until it cracked softly, and dismissed her weapon.

"Not bad, you two," she said to the twins.

"Do you think they know we're here now?" asked Gideon.

"I don't think so. Feel that?" Tim opened his senses and could feel a great deal of distant elemental energies. He nodded; whatever was making that was probably too distracted to sense them. But what could cause…

"Mom," Tim said quietly, "look up."

They all did. The reddish glow that suffused the copse had not been just from the *utari*. The sky was lit up a lurid orange-red. A flickering orange-red.

"That's no sunset," she whispered, and took off running through the trees. The teens followed in her wake, and nearly ran into her at the grove's end.

"No," she said softly, "oh no, Vic, no."

Forestview was on fire.

Chapter 21

Smoke poured from half a dozen windows on the top floor of the building, while flickers of orange danced on the roof. A multitude of emergency vehicles surrounded the main entrance, their lights pulsing red and blue, while a hook-and-ladder jetted water into one of the windows. A crowd of doctors, patients, and staff stood nearby, watching. Looking at the flames, Tim felt his palms become greasy, and an elastic band seemed to snug down around his chest.

Annika turned to him, her forehead creased with worry. "Honey, are you sure you're going to be okay?"

"Yeah." Tim licked his lips and stared at the building. "I got this."

"With so many people here," said Vee, "how are we going to get in?"

"That actually makes it easier," said Annika. "Come here." She started weaving, a ridiculously complicated pattern of Earth and Air, then touched her palm to each of their foreheads. A wave of cold trickled down Tim's body, like someone poured a glass of ice water on his head. He looked at his companions but saw no difference.

"What did that do?"

"Invisibility is almost impossible," his mom explained, "but blending in? Easier than you'd think." She held her arms out to her sides, expectantly. "Well?

C'mon, I can't do it on myself."

"Who, me?"

"No, my other ridiculously talented son. I know you were paying attention."

"Okay." Tim drew in Earth and Air and began layering the weave, holding the effect and what he'd seen Annika doing. Suddenly the logic of the weave clicked in his mind. Perhaps if he also added Water...

"No," she interrupted, "leave that Air. Water is the element of emotion, while Air is associated with intellect. Those are professionals over there, people doing a job. Water in that weave would work better in a more passionate situation, like a sporting event or a concert."

"That makes a lot of sense, actually." He completed the weave and then touched his mother's forehead. She shivered slightly, then nodded.

"Alright, let's go." Annika turned toward the entrance.

The ease with which they entered the building was almost laughable. Annika simply walked up to an ambulance, pulled a gurney out of the back, and started unfolding it. The EMT sitting in the back gave her only the most cursory of glances before going back to his prep work. The four of them each took a corner of the gurney and rolled it through the crowd, people parting as though they belonged there. One policewoman made eye contact with Tim, and before he could look away, she gave him a quick, respectful nod, as if to say *Glad you're here.*

"What are they seeing?" he stage-whispered to his mom.

"Whatever they think they should see." She spoke

casually, making no attempt to lower her voice. "That's how the weave works. It simply amplifies the viewer's expectations. I only grabbed the gurney because an EMT crew are the most likely people to enter a burning building."

As soon as they passed Forestview's security station, they ditched the gurney and made for the stairs, not trusting the elevator. The stairway was deserted, the only light coming from the emergency floods and a single fire alarm on the ceiling strobing a sharp double-flash every few seconds. As they made their way up, the temperature rose significantly and strands of smoke hung in the air, the sharp, acrid smell making the phobic knot in Tim's chest tighten down. By the time they reached the fourth-floor landing, they had to weave filters of Air to cover their faces in order to see and breathe clearly. Annika reached out and quickly touched the door, obviously feeling for heat. She looked back at the others.

"Ready?"

All three teens nodded, and she opened the door.

If the stairway was stifling, the fourth floor was an oven. Sweat immediately popped out on Tim's forehead, and his breath came in short bursts, amplified in his own ears by the filter weave. The floodlights here cut bright cones through the haze, but at the end of the long hall they could see a lurid, flickering glow, and the entire ceiling was obscured by a cloud of muddy brown smoke. Annika gestured with her head for Tim to take the lead, her features set and her mouth a tight line. He opened his senses and started forward, the twins flanking him left and right. Annika turned to ease the door shut behind them.

A wave of cold chills shot down Tim's spine.

He had just enough time to throw up a shield before a blast of blue-black flames roared out of a nearby door. It broke on Tim's barrier like a wave, sucking the air from the corridor and making the skin on his face feel tight and stretched, then rolled past. In its wake, stepped a figure in black, slender and of a height with Tim, wearing a hood and with a mask pulled up to cover their features. From behind came at least a half-dozen *vrolachi*.

"You!" The figure stared at Tim with bald hatred.

"Last time I checked, yeah." Tim smirked. He twisted his barrier into a column and flung it at them. It came at them like a rolling log, undercutting the Murks and spilling them to the floor, but the Midnighter jumped lithely over it, weaving Fire and Darkness into twin blades in their hands. Tim wove his own weapons, police batons of Air and Water glowing faintly blue, and let his combat weave fall into place. They clashed, dancing and weaving, weapons throwing off multi-colored sparks, only vaguely aware of the other battles going on around them. Tim's opponent attacked with a blind fury, driving him backward. He stumbled and lost his footing, but just as he was about to be impaled, the Midnighter flew sideways, crashed into the wall, and stuck there. Annika stalked past Tim, aiglos upraised. A Murk appeared from the shadows and tried to pounce, but without turning she held out a hand. The *vrolach* stopped in mid-air, hung for a moment, then burst into flames. Annika tilted her head and regarded the trapped Midnighter.

"Don't touch my son," she said, almost conversationally.

"I care nothing for what you want, Corruptor!" To Tim's surprise, the voice was feminine. As if to confirm, his mother gestured twice and his opponent's hood and mask flipped off, revealing a pale, heart-shaped face and a thick, coppery braid of hair. She would have been quite pretty if not for the rage and disgust twisting her features.

"I have just two questions for you," Annika continued. "Where is Naldumiel, and where is my husband?"

As if in answer, the wall thirty feet down the corridor exploded outward, carrying with it a broad, heavy figure in a long coat, holding a staff. He rolled into a crouch far quicker than his bulk would imply, one hand on the ground, staff held out stiffly behind him, ready to counterattack.

And out through the gaping hole in the corridor wall stalked Victor Hansen.

Chapter 22

Despite his own fear, Tim's heart surged with excitement. Gone was the drugged, passive version of his father. Vic stood tall and clear-eyed, an expression of anger and disappointment on his still-whiskered face. Elemental power came off of him in waves, and Tim was unsurprised to find that he was nearly as strong as Annika.

"That was sloppy, Dume." Vic picked his way across the rubble. "Did you really think I wouldn't be ready for you?"

"I had no idea what sort of substances those doctors may have pumped into you." Naldumiel straightened as he spoke. "For all I knew you could have been sitting in the corner blowing spit bubbles."

"You know better." He glanced down the hallway and noticed his family for the first time. A look of confusion crossed his face.

"Annika," he muttered, "what...why are you..."

"The Ban is broken, Vittorio," said Naldumiel. "Do you remember?"

"The Ban." Vic turned away, his brow furrowed. "How long?"

"Sixteen years," said Annika. She started toward Vic, but Naldumiel snapped his staff out, leveled at her chest.

"*You* need to stay out of this!" he snarled.

"Do not threaten me," she replied evenly, and Tim felt the air around her crackle.

"I am not threatening you!" Tim could see frustration woven with real fear on the Midnighter's face. "You have no idea what you are doing. *Let me handle this.*"

"STOP!"

Everyone's eyes snapped to Vic. He was staring, eyes wide but distant, at Tim.

"T-Timothy?" His voice was soft, shaky, unbelieving. "Timothy, how can…you're so…" He dug his hands into his hair and turned away.

Naldumiel grabbed Tim tightly by his upper arm and pulled him close. "Tim, listen, you need to leave, you need to get out of sight *right now.*"

"Get your hands off my son!" Annika lashed out with a weave of Air, trying to separate the two of them, but the Midnighter severed it and turned to her.

"You idiot, you have no idea the damage you're causing!" He turned back to Tim. "Please, there's no time to explain."

At that moment, a flash of blue-white swung down toward the two of them. Naldumiel turned and raised his staff just in time to parry a blow from Annika's spear. He released Tim and counterattacked with shocking speed for a man of his bulk, driving her back with a flurry of spinning blows. Tim moved to intervene, but a blast of Darkness blindsided him, knocking him to the ground. The female Midnighter stood over him, a satisfied smirk on her face.

"Now, where were we?" She wove, and a long black blade appeared in her hand.

"NO!" A slim figure tackled her, her weapon

falling from her hand and dissolving. They rolled together, flailing and kicking, then flung apart under the force of an Air blast from one of them. They both landed on their feet, poised and ready, and the girl Nightweaver flickered a glance at Tim.

"Go to your dad, dude," said a voice behind Tim, and Gideon stepped forward, holding a massive cudgel woven of Earth and Fire. "We got this one."

The twins converged on the Midnighter, but Tim had already turned, scrambling up and running toward the hole in the corridor wall. His father knelt there amongst the chunks of drywall and cinderblock, his head down and both hands knotted in his hair, rocking back and forth.

"Dad?" Tim skidded to a halt and crouched down, putting a hand on Vic's shoulder. The older man jumped and looked up at him, eyes wide and frightened. "Dad, we gotta go. Can you stand up?"

"You," Vic muttered softly, and his expression softened, "you're my Timothy."

"Yeah, Daddy," Tim felt his throat constrict and his eyes sting, "it's me, but we need to go."

"But you can't be. Timothy is just a baby, and you're so tall." His gaze went to the scars on Tim's face, and his eyebrows knotted together. He reached out and, ever so gently, touched Tim's cheek. "The fire. I hurt you."

"I'm okay, Dad. It was an accident, and that was a long time ago."

"But I would never hurt you." He lowered his head again and closed his eyes. "There's too much…too much in my *mind*."

"Tim, no!" cried Naldumiel. "You have to get

away from him!" A gout of fire distracted him. Further down, the girl Midnighter and the twins danced a deadly dance.

"It's okay, let's get you someplace safe."

"I would never hurt you, I would never hurt my boy." Vic began to rock back and forth again, his voice getting higher and more strange. "I would never hurt my Timothy, I would never hurt my boy, I would never hurt him, I would never hurt my boy."

"Dad, please." Tim knelt and tried to put an arm around his father when Vic suddenly stiffened. His head snapped up and his gaze drilled into Tim, flat and hard and full of malice.

"You are not my son."

The blast of energy from Vic threw Tim the length of the hallway and knocked everyone else off their feet. Had Tim not been able to throw a simple shield of Air around himself, the impact against the far wall would have broken every bone in his body. As it was, he lay stunned for a moment, head ringing like a struck bell. He heard shouting, and felt the now-familiar crawling of someone weaving Darkness. He raised his head and saw his father at the center of a cyclone of power, the others shielding their eyes, calling out to him.

"Vic, no!" cried Annika.

"You have to listen to me, Vittorio," called Naldumiel over the tumult, "we're here to help you!"

"Anukh vas mauzan buth," chanted Vic, his hands held out in front of him, *"bokav rho mubulat agh flakh!"* The words rang strangely in Tim's mind. A staff of polished bone appeared in Vic's hand. He whirled it above his head and slammed the butt of it down onto the floor, channeling all the elemental fury

around him into it. A circle of blackness spread out from the point of impact, like ripples in a pool, and a foul, thick smell filled the corridor.

"No!" Naldumiel stumbled back from the spreading darkness. "A *pyrkagia* will kill us all!"

"No," said Vic softly, "just all of you."

Something reached up out of the black circle, an arm or limb as thick as a tree, with scales the color of old blood and claws as long as Tim's forearm. It grasped the outer edge of the circle and heaved, revealing a head out of nightmares: a massive fanged jaw, ram-like horns framing an oddly flat face with only slits for a nose, and tiny, too-far apart eyes glowing a bright, electric blue and filled with dark intelligence. It fixed Tim with its gaze and seemed to grin.

A flash of light exploded between them, and both recoiled. The *pyrkagia* bellowed like an alligator and clawed its way out completely, revealing vestigial wings and the hindquarters of a great cat, its head nearly brushing the ceiling. A weave of Air caught Tim around the waist and yanked him backward, just in time to avoid a swipe of the demon's claws. He skidded to a halt with his back against the wall, and looked up to see everyone, Dusker and Midnighter alike, gazing down the hallway at the beast.

"Sit this one out, kiddo," said Annika, "we got this." And they all charged.

Tim had thought seeing Vee and Gideon fight together was impressive, but it was nothing compared to the full assault of five trained willworkers. Their combined attack drove the *pyrkagia* sideways, crashing it into and through the already-weakened wall, but this only seemed to enrage it. It bellowed again and pounced, moving with incredible speed for something so large, but everyone sidestepped with the unnatural grace combat weaves gave. In the shadows behind the fight, Tim saw his father smiling grimly and still holding his staff. He saw Tim and his expression changed, recognition warring with anger and confusion for a moment. Then he called out in the same, guttural language he'd used before, just as a blast of fire from Annika caught the beast full in the face, driving it back and around. Enraged by the assault, it turned on Vic and attacked.

"No!" Tim saw his father fly into the wall and slump like a rag doll. He ran forward, drawing hard, harder than he ever had, driven by panic and anger. Just as the demon reared to attack Vic again, Tim twisted all the energies into a single, massive attack and released. Arcs of scarlet lightning streamed from his outstretched hands, enveloping the *pyrkagia*. It screamed, a strangely high-pitched sound after all of its grunts and rumbles, and stumbled sideways, trying in vain to bat the assault away. The others took advantage. Blue-black flames gouted from the end of Naldumiel's staff; a pipe in the ceiling burst, the water twisting into a spray of stinging ice from Vee; a series of shockwaves from Gideon destabilized the floor. To Tim's surprise, the Midnighter girl rushed forward through the chaos to his father's side.

"Pour it on!" Annika dashed forward, raining blows of her spear on its forelegs. Screaming again, the *pyrkagia* tried to rear up, its horned head crashing through the ceiling tiles. She ducked beneath it, driving her aiglos upward and bracing the butt against the floor, and its full weight came down, driving the blade deep.

"Get clear!" To Tim's surprise, Naldumiel caught her around the waist with the same weave she'd used on him and pulled her away, just as a river of liquid fire burst from the demon's wound. It hit the floor and began to eat away at it like acid. The beast shrieked and flailed, pawing at the spear still embedded in its guts. The flames spread, engulfing the *pyrkagia* itself, causing it to convulse more. Naldumiel ran to the other Midnighter, who was trying to drag Vic's inert form away from the chaos.

"We have to get clear!" Annika grabbed Tim's arm and shoved him toward the stairs. "That thing's blood is going to eat right through—"

A fifty-foot section of the hallway collapsed, taking the burning *pyrkagia* with it. It gave one last howl of agony, then a geyser of fire erupted out of the hole. Panic screamed in Tim's mind, but he managed to weave the blast away from himself. He crouched and squeezed his eyes shut, fighting the urge to run screaming from the wall of heat. The roar faded, but Tim remained where he was, head down, hands over his ears, trembling.

"Tim?"

Get up, said the rational part of his brain.

Nope, said another, deeper part. *No way, there are fires out there, ain't movin'.*

"Tim, get up," his mother said. "The fires are spreading, and Vee's hurt."

"What?" That cut through the haze of fear. Tim opened his eyes and saw his worst nightmare. The center of the hallway was an inferno, broken masonry, tiles, and chunks of ceiling surrounded a gaping hole like a portal to hell. Billowing smoke and tongues of fire blocked the view of the other side of the corridor and swept upward through a matching hole in the ceiling, offering a glimpse of the cloudy night sky.

"I can't find the Midnighters or your dad." Tim turned to see Annika, sooty and disheveled but unhurt. Nearby, Gideon knelt by the prone figure of Vee, a nasty gash across her forehead, the swirl of healing weaves surrounding both of them.

"I tried to suppress the flames, but it's not working. I think," —she hesitated— "I think you can probably do it better than I can."

Tim understood. He got to his feet and reached out for that strange, underneath element he'd sensed when the *vrolachi* had him. It was there immediately, flat, cold, yet strangely vital. He drew and intertwined it with Fire and Air, and spread it across the flaming abyss. As he did, a giddy, almost lightheaded thrill ran through him. The fire seemed to fight him, like a pack of dogs pulling on a single leash, but then subsided, revealing a pair of figures on the other side.

"Naldumiel!" cried Annika.

The Midnighter turned, and Tim could see through the smoke that he had Vic draped over his shoulder in a fireman's carry. His companion glared at Tim across the divide.

"Your fault," he cried over the tumult of the fire. "All of this, all of this unnecessary pain and destruction, I lay it all at your feet, Annika."

"Bring him back to me, or I swear…"

"Why? So you can finish destroying him? No, not this time." He muttered something to his companion and turned to walk away.

"Hold the fire down, Tim," Annika muttered

through clenched teeth. She took three steps back and started weaving Air, but at the same time the female Midnighter held her hand out over the pit and started chanting in the same guttural language Vic had used. Tim's skin crawled.

"Mom, don't!" But it was too late. She sprinted forward and leapt into the air, propelling herself up with her weave. Just as she cleared the edge, a fiery hand the size of a garbage can lid reached up from the inferno and swatted her out of the air. Annika rebounded off the side wall, fell hard, and lay still.

"MOM!" As Tim moved towards her, a searing pain blasted through his head, causing him to stumble and fall to his knees. He lost his grip on the weave containing the fire, and it flared back to life, obscuring the Midnighters again, but not before he saw the girl smiling triumphantly at him. He tried to get to his feet, but another burning hand slammed to the ground just inches from him, and then another, making him scuttle backward. Four *utari* clambered up out of the flames.

"Tim, run!" It was Vee, on her feet, looking unsteady. Gideon was already lifting Annika onto his broad shoulder. Tim threw one last, desperate glance behind him and bolted toward the stairwell.

As the twins made their way down, Tim hesitated just long enough to yank the door shut and twist a quick weave of Fire into the latch to fuse it. Just as he finished, something slammed into the other side, rattling the door in its frame and sending puffs of sparks through the cracks around the jam, scorching Tim's sleeve. He batted at them as he ran down, taking the steps two at a time. Another blow hit the door above, harder this time. He had just enough time to make it to the first landing before the *utari* blew open the door with enough force to shatter the hinges and send it sliding down the stairs after them like a sled. The fire-spirits followed, flowing like liquid in order to fit through the frame, closing the distance with sickening ease.

"Go, go, go!" Tim started leaping down the stairs, trusting the combat weave would give him the reflexes to not turn an ankle. He threw weaves of Water and Earth blindly behind him, just trying to slow the *utari*, the phobia-panic nibbling at the edges of his mind. Ahead, Vee reached the first floor doorway and hurled an Air weave at it, blowing it open just in time for them to leap through.

"What the... WOAH!"

The four of them collapsed on the floor right at the feet of a squad of firefighters preparing to enter the stairway. A blast of heat followed them, but oddly the *utari* did not. They cowered just inside the doorway, looking like nothing so much as a pile of burning debris.

"*Hose!*" one of the firefighters shouted, and a blast of water shot over their heads and into the stairwell. A massive, hissing screech echoed out, and the truth dawned on Tim. Just as he could not weave blatantly in front of Sleepers, supernatural creatures must not be able to take their true form in front of them either. The fire-spirits could do nothing in front of them but be destroyed by the spray from the hose.

"Are you alright?" A strong hand held Tim's elbow and helped him to his feet. Behind the oxygen mask, the firefighter's eyes were focused but respectful, and Tim realized his mom's disguising weave must still be in place.

"We're fine," Tim answered, thinking quickly, "but we think there might be some people trapped on the fourth floor. Be careful, a section of hallway has collapsed up there." He reached into the weave he could now feel clinging to his skin, drew in a trickle of energy, and *pushed*.

"Yes, sir!" The firefighter turned to the others. "You heard the man. Up to four, we have people to save! Let's move!" And without another question they started up the stairs, boots crunching over the remains of the soaked *utari*.

"Lay her down over here," said Vee, and Tim turned to see Gideon easing his mother to the floor. Vee knelt and wove, while Tim stood to one side, watching and worrying. He could see the scorch marks all down her right side, and there was blood in her hair, near enough to where she'd been hurt in the accident that worrisome images flitted through his mind. Then with a gasp, Annika sat up, startling the teens. She looked around wildly.

"No," she said, and tried to get to her feet. "No, we have to go back, why did you bring me down here? We have to go back up."

"Mom, you have to lay still." He went to her and crouched down.

She grabbed the front of his shirt. "No, you don't understand!" Tears shone in her eyes. "You don't know what they're going to do to him, I do! We have to go back up while there's still time!"

"They're gone, Mom." Tim felt his own throat tighten. "We had to get away. You were down, Vee was hurt, and they sent those fire-things after us. We had to run, and by now—"

"No." She shook her head slowly. "We have to try. Do you know what they are going to do to your father?"

"Most likely," said a deep, masculine voice behind them, "no more than what he deserves."

Tim spun and saw a semicircle of people standing in the foyer behind them, all dressed in the same, military-like gray outfits that Annika wore. In the center was a massive man, well over six feet tall with broad, muscular shoulders, glossy black hair pulled back in a ponytail, a neat beard streaked with gray, and a large, hawkish nose. A very familiar nose.

"Dad?" said Vee.

Chapter 23

Meneleas' gaze flicked toward his children, then back to Annika. He looked grim and more than a little uncomfortable. Tim's mom, on the other hand, managed a small, sad smile.

"Hey, Mel," she said simply. "The kids got big."

"You know why we're here," he said in a tight voice.

"I'm surprised it took this long." She tried to stand and stumbled. Tim rushed to her side and caught her, but the rest of the surrounding Duskers tensed up, as though expecting an attack. Their leader alone did not move.

"Why now, Nika, after all this time?"

"I didn't have much choice." She winced and hobbled forward, her arm slung across Tim's shoulder. "Between your kids sticking their noses into our lives and Naldumiel showing up." The rest of the semicircle looked around nervously, as though they expected the Midnighter to pop up out of thin air.

"Is he still here?" Meneleas' scowl darkened.

"No." The heartbreak in that single word from Annika was palpable. Tim pulled her closer and she leaned her head against his chest.

"I take no pleasure in doing this," Meneleas said softly.

"I know." She looked up at him. "Do what you

need to do."

"Annika no Titania Serafi," he said in a ringing tone, "sixteen years ago, you violated the most sacred laws of the Children of Dusk. You consorted with our ancient enemy and committed high treason upon your people. You escaped justice and, with the help of individuals we shall not name here, went into self-imposed exile from the Duskrealms and from Opacaroi society. The Ban of the Lethe was placed upon you at this time, concealing your whereabouts and effectively making your exile complete. Is everything I have stated correct."

"Yes," said Annika.

"It was decided in your absence that, as long as the Ban held, your punishment was sufficient and no further action would be taken upon you or your family until and unless such time came as to make it unavoidable." His gaze went briefly to Tim. "The Ban has since been broken, and you and your family have interacted with Opacaroi society once more, violating the terms and allowances of your exile. The Gray Council has issued a warrant for your immediate arrest. You will accompany us to Avalon to stand trial for your crimes."

"What?" cried Tim.

"Hush," said Annika, soft but strong.

"Will you come with us willingly to face judgment, or do you intend to resist?" The tension in the room ratcheted up significantly. *They're afraid,* Tim thought. *They're afraid of my mother.* She gave a small sigh.

"What would be the point?" The surrounding Duskers visibly relaxed.

"You will relinquish your aiglos," Meneleas

continued. "Any attempt to summon it to your person will be considered an act of aggression and will result in the harshest of consequences. Do you understand?"

Annika nodded and held out her hand. Although the last time Tim had seen the spear it had gone into the abyss, still embedded in the guts of the *pyrkagia*, her aiglos appeared in a swirl of blue light. Another Dusker, a slender man with pale, thinning hair and a sharp, angular face, started forward as though he expected to take the weapon, but instead Meneleas took it reverently. As he did, his grim facade cracked for a moment, revealing real regret and pain underneath. He glanced back at another of the group, and gestured with his head. A woman with a lined, stern face and a strong, athletic build started forward, reaching into a pack she had slung across her shoulders. As she approached, her eyes met Annika's, and Tim saw some sort of wordless conversation pass between the two women. From the bag, she pulled what looked to be a set of wide, interconnected bracelets of some dark metal, like tarnished brass. Annika hesitated, then unslung her arm from around Tim's shoulder. She held out her hands, palms down and fingers together, and the woman slipped the bracelets on her. They contracted, shrinking in size until they fit snugly around her wrists, and she gasped.

"Are they hurting you?" Tim made to reach for them, but she pulled away.

"No, I'm fine. They're called binding bands. They block the ability to weave." She gave Tim that same, sad smile. "They don't hurt, but they're not pleasant to wear."

"Genevieve no Seriah Corvitae, come forward,"

said Meneleas. Vee approached her father, head high and shoulders square, Gideon trailing just behind. "The terms of your assignment were to work as a Seeker, remaining outside the Duskrealms other than for required contact for a period of two years, or until you discovered a potential willworker who could be introduced to Opacaroi society. While the introduction was, shall we say, unorthodox, you have clearly fulfilled the requirements. You shall accompany us back to Avalon to. . . continue your life where you left off." The hesitation in Meneleas' voice caught Tim's ear, and he noticed Vee stiffen at the same moment.

"Fulfilled the requirements, did she?" It was the sharp-featured man who moved to take the aiglos.

"The boy has inherited his mother's brilliance, Nikolos" said the stern-faced woman, "that much has already been documented by Kieran."

"The question is not what he got from his mother's side of the family, Josefea," Nikolos replied, "but from his father."

"A *question*," cut in Meneleas, clearly annoyed, "that will be addressed by the full Council, not by us in the lobby of a burning hospital." He then turned and regarded Tim. "Which brings us to our last piece of business here."

"Is that what I am to you," snapped Tim, "a piece of business?"

"For the time being, yes." His face remained stern, but Tim thought he caught a flicker of something else in the older Dusker's eyes. Amusement? "Timoteo ko Vittorio Serafi, we have been in contact with Argent House and know of your potential. We request that you also accompany us to Avalon."

"Request?" Tim felt his temper rise. "You're arresting my mom, my friends are going with you, my dad is who knows where, and I have no other family. How is this a request?"

"That's not entirely true," said Josefea.

"What do you mean?"

"Do you want to tell him, Nika?" The older woman smiled at Tim's mom.

"Kiddo, this is your great-aunt Josefea. Aunt Jo, this is my son, Tim."

Tim was floored, but it made sense. Why wouldn't he have family in the Duskrealms? As he looked at the two women smiling at him, he could now see a strong resemblance, especially in the eyes and mouth.

"A very touching family reunion," said Nikolos, "but I think, Meneleas, that—"

"...that this is not the place to undertake this discussion." Meneleas stared pointedly at the smaller man, who held his gaze for a beat before lowering his eyes.

"Yes, First Speaker."

"Duskers," Meneleas barked, "fall in! Pietro, Matea, go begin the preparations. Michel, Landon, Simeon, scout upstairs and make sure there's no sign of the Mitternachten and their thralls. And help the firefighters if you can." Five of the surrounding Duskers took off in different directions. He then eyed Josefea and Nikolos. "I suppose the two of you should escort Annika. Ariela, please accompany Tim."

"Who's Ariela?"

"That would be me," said a voice behind Tim. He turned and saw a tall, dark-skinned girl no older than the twins, her hair in tight cornrows, and the most astonishing eyes Tim had ever seen on a person; wide and round and as gold as a cat's. Eyes that stared at Tim with bald dislike.

"Alright, let's move." They gathered into a loose group, with Tim, Annika, and their escorts in the center. His mom shot Tim a tight, brittle smile, and he could tell she was at the end of her endurance. As if on cue, Josefea placed a hand on the side of her niece's face and started weaving. It seemed that, while those bands might keep someone from weaving themselves, it still allowed healing to work, for Tim could see the angry burns on his mother's arm already visibly fading.

The group went straight out the front doors, and he assumed they must be using that same disguising weave, because no one interfered with them as they made their way toward the grove. Tim glanced back and saw the fire trucks dousing the gaping hole in Forestview's roof left by the death of the *pyrkagia*. His stomach tightened at the thought of his father. Where was he? What punishment would he undergo at the hands of his people? Tim swore silently to himself that, no matter what, he would find out the truth of his dad's fate, and save him if he could.

The group reached the same grove where Tim, Annika and the twins had arrived, and he saw two Duskers there, weaving something massive, something that made the air between them flex and distort like a heat mirage. Meneleas approached the distortion and held out a hand. To Tim's surprise, an aiglos appeared in it, one very different from his mother's: steel gray edged with soft gold, like sunlight filtering through storm clouds. He set the haft of the spear on the ground between his feet, lowered his head, and drew. Tim's arms crawled with goosebumps, and he was unsurprised to find that Meneleas was indeed strong, at least as strong as his father. The air before him seemed to twist and tear apart, revealing a flat black hole rippling with color at the edges like oil on a pond. Without hesitating, Meneleas stepped through and vanished, followed by the rest of the entourage. Tim swallowed.

"Nervous?" asked Ariela.

"Yeah," Tim replied.

"You should be," she said, not unkindly, but she did not smile. They stepped through together.

The two Duskers holding the portal released their weaves and stepped through. It shimmered on its own for a heartbeat, then crumpled in on itself soundlessly and disappeared in a brief flash of blue light. The grove stood deserted and dark, except for the strobe from the distant emergency lights and the glow of the dying fire.

A word about the author...

James C. Struck is an author and musician who writes modern and high fantasy, speculative fiction, New Age philosophy, poetry, and every kind of music under the sun. He holds a BA in Music Theory and Composition from Columbia College Chicago and is active in local community theater. James is happily married with three amazing kids and lives in the Illinois River Valley area. He is also the author of the children's book The Curious Snowflake: A Parable. Children of Dusk is his first published novel.

JamesCStruck.com

www.ingramcontent.com/pod-product-compliance
Lightning Source LLC
Chambersburg PA
CBHW070112030726
47506CB00002B/700